ELEVEN SOOTY DREAMS

Manuela Draeger

Translated from the
French by
J.T. Mahany

OPEN LETTER

LITERARY TRANSLATIONS FROM THE UNIVERSITY OF ROCHESTER

Library of Congress Cataloging-in-Publication Data: Available.
ISBN-13: 978-1-948830-26-3 / ISBN-10: 1-948830-26-4

This work received support from the French Ministry of Foreign Affairs and the Cultural Services of the French Embassy in the United States through their publishing assistance program.

This project is supported in part by an award from the National Endowment for the Arts and the New York State Council on the Arts with the support of Governor Andrew M. Cuomo and the New York State Legislature.

Printed on acid-free paper in the United States of America.

Cover Design by Jenny Volvovski
Interior Design by Anthony Blake

Open Letter is the University of Rochester's nonprofit, literary translation press:
Dewey Hall 1-219, Box 278968, Rochester, NY 14627

www.openletterbooks.org

ELEVEN SOOTY DREAMS

Bolcho Pride

1.

Your name is Imayo Özbeg. You are burning. I go to you. My memories are yours.

Your name is Imayo Özbeg. We were raised in the same barracks. You are burning. I go to you. In this moment we are all moving toward you. My memories are yours.

Your name is Imayo Özbeg, and we have always considered each other members of the same family. We share in our heads images of the same street, with its barbed-wire-covered doors and its corridors open sometimes to darkness, sometimes to the silent pain of the poor, sometimes to nothing. We went to the same school. We were raised by the same grandmothers, the same uncles and aunts, and, for several years, we slept in the same barracks. In the company of adults, we regularly marched in the Bolshevik Pride parade. This year things went poorly. You are burning. I go to you. In this moment, we are with you. We are all moving toward you. We are exchanging our last breaths. Your memory trickles from your eyes. My memories are yours.

Your name is Imayo Özbeg, and, if one wishes to meet you, one must wander for a bit in the Amaniyak Kree district, in the center of the Negrini Bloc. From now on, to see you and speak to you, I will have to wander once more, but this will be after a long journey in another world, and there is no indication that this world exists. We have always considered each other members of the same family. We share in our heads images of the same street, with its barbed-wire-covered doors and its corridors open sometimes to darkness, sometimes to the silent pain of the poor, sometimes to nothing. The streets have numbers, but we preferred to give them the names of our heroes and heroines, the names of our dragons, the names of our martyrs. Adiyana Soledad, Leel Fourmanova, Iada Thünal, Ravial Mawash, Domar Dong.

We went to the same school, across from the Doumna Tathaï barracks. You were good friends with my little brother. For two years, you sat at the same desk. We were raised by the same grandmothers, the same uncles and aunts, and, for several years, we slept in the same barracks. In the company of adults, we regularly marched in the Bolshevik Pride parade. When I go back very far in my memory, when I direct myself toward the fog that precedes conscious childhood, I see that I have retained the images of the demonstrations and the festival. Deformed, fragmentary, reinvented, but I've held onto them. It's true that in our gray daily lives, they were like sudden explosions of color. Every year, around the middle of October, the Bolshevik Pride festival, also known as Bolcho Pride, took place. Try to remember how it illuminated our childhood. With all the other families from the neighboring ghettos, we joined the flood of people going to participate in the festivities. Big and small, no one avoided having a good time, and it was even the one moment, in twelve months' time, when we'd hear laughter cascade everywhere around us. This year things went poorly, Bolcho Pride was a festival of violence and pain.

You are burning. I go to you. In this moment, we are with you.
We all move toward you. We are exchanging our last breaths.
Your memory trickles from your eyes.
My memories are yours.

Your name is Imayo Özbeg, and, if one wishes to meet you, one must wander for a bit in the Amaniyak Kree neighborhood, in the center of the Negrini Bloc. From now on, to see you and speak to you, I will have to wander once more, but this will be after a long journey in another world, and there is no indication that this world exists. Whether you remain unattainable there, lock yourself away there like a sick wolf, or to the contrary hope for many visitors, it will be difficult to find you. We all know that between us there will soon be awful and uncrossable ravines. From the moment we are extinguished, multiple obstacles will separate us. But let's not talk about the future. Let's not talk about the uncertain and incomprehensible. Let's talk about our past, let's examine one last time the years when we were, when we are together.

Let's talk about our childhood. We have always considered each other members of the same family. We share in our heads images of the same street, with its barbed-wire-covered doors and it corridors open sometimes to darkness, sometimes to the silent pain of the poor, sometimes to nothing. The streets have numbers, but we preferred to give them the names of our heroes and heroines, the names of our dragons, the names of our martyrs. Adiyana Soledad Street, Leel Fourmanova Street, Iada Thünal Alley, Ravial Mawash Boulevard, Domar Dong Crossing.

We went to the same school, across from the Doumna Tathaï barracks. You were good friends with my little brother. In elementary school, we shared the same desk. We were raised by the same grandmothers, the same uncles and aunts, and, for several years, we slept in the same barracks. In the company of adults, we regularly marched in the Bolshevik Pride parade. When I go back very far in my memory, when I direct myself toward the fog that precedes conscious childhood, I see that I have retained the images of the demonstrations and the festival. Deformed, fragmentary, reinvented, but I've held onto them. It's true that in our gray daily lives, they were like sudden explosions of color, and that even a baby could tell the difference between the two.

Every year, around the middle of October, the Bolshevik Pride festival, also known as Bolcho Pride, took place. Try to remember how it illuminated our childhood. With all the other families from the neighboring ghettos, we joined the flood of people going to participate in the festivities. Big and small, everyone gave in to the revelry, and it was the one moment, in twelve months' time, when we'd hear laughter cascade everywhere around us.

Bolcho Pride was technically forbidden, but there were so many of us that the police on that day laid low, kept their distance, and only intervened at the moment of dispersion, when our best and brightest began expressing their rage with Molotov cocktails, or by lynching several informers or spies. I must also say that, at the time, the authorities already considered us to be inoffensive vestiges, absurd remnants of the past, mothballed and ridiculous fossils, and they accorded us the right to demonstrate in order to channel our bitterness, as well as, I think, to update their files on subversive elements, and to evaluate the state of our forces. On the path of our immense parade, or strolling between the stands, we would often come across suspicious-looking tourists, dressed like everyone else in military tatters, but outfitted with high-end cameras or miniaturized camcorders. These are the people who get disemboweled at the end of the parade, who don't have the intelligence to hide in time. Our Komsomols don't give them a chance, and, to tell the truth, especially today when we've lost several of our own, I don't pity them at all.

When I evoke Bolcho Pride, and I suppose your impressions and mine overlap, I first of all remember imprecise images from my childhood, memories of madness crossed between legs and knees, I remember the enormous, uninterrupted rumble of marching demonstrators. When I fall, I am caught. When I am tired, someone lifts me up onto their shoulders, an uncle, my father, I do not know. From my unbalanced perch, having to lean against hair smelling of sweat and damp wood so as not to slide off, I tower over the outpouring of the masses. My uncle or my father, or an adult belonging to this broad category, holds me by an ankle, his other hand busy directing cries of rage, fist closed, at the sky and the capitalists. I don't understand a word of what the multitude is shouting. I cling tight to my carrier's forehead. I'm a little afraid of this thundering tide surrounding me. I'm afraid of suddenly falling to the ground and being trampled by the proletarian legions. The fear excites me. I let out shouts of my own, shrill cries meant more for myself than the enemy. I'm beside myself.

I then find more recent images, tied to an age when I had already claimed language and when, doubtlessly, I must have possessed my first thoughts of egalitarian ideology. I remember being electrified with emotion the evening before, as I unwrapped the clothes the adults had given me for the next day. Most of the time, my existence as a little girl was ignored and I was dressed like Dzerzhinsky. I was proud to wear a felt military helmet and put on a false goatee and mustache. My little brother regularly received a Chapayev costume. He never complained about having to play the role of such a celebrated, heroically red individual during the festival, but he did put forward a few doubts on the pillbox cap that was thrust onto his head, and that, cobbled together by Granny Holgolde or one of the other grandmothers out of swatches of old blanket, poorly recreated the magnificent original worn by the commander of the Twenty-Fifth Division, made of black lambskin. My little brother thought his cap wasn't as stylish as my helmet, and his disappointment was obvious when he compared his simple black mustache to my Dzerzhinskian pilosity, which was less thick, but twice the length. Like good comrades, we often traded our symbols of these implacable leaders, and, very quickly, our disguises deteriorated. We became hybrids more carnivalesque than revolutionary, for which the adults didn't dare reproach us. We were little. They bent down to caress us and fix the bands keeping our masks in place. Sometimes they uttered a few joyful remarks on the beginnings of the Cheka or the machine guns of the Ural. But, most of the time, they were content to affectionately encourage us to grow up and carry on. As advice goes, this was a bit vague, but I think we understood what they meant: fidelity to the cause of the vanquished, the pursuit of combat regardless of the irreversibility of defeat, enthusiasm in thinking about lost opportunities. We were going to grow up and, until our deaths, hold high the flags of all these disasters.

The festive agitation took hold of nearly everyone we knew, children and adults, manics and depressives, bigmouthed chatterboxes as well as the rebellious-faced taciturn. Bolcho Pride, the great people's demonstration, its roaring surge, was approaching. For a week or two, the mood of the family environment and the ghetto changed. Despondency was placed between two parentheses. The feeling of having no future was dimmed. We were all suddenly certain of our belonging to a community of brave souls, valiant, lucid, optimistic proletarians, on the point of being led to something luminous that would break our millenary habits of collapse, enslavement, and defeat. From one house to the next, people could be heard calling out to each other differently, their voices seemingly perked up by the imminence of a new insurrectional fraternity. Songs would ring out at any given moment, coming for example from the crystal sets that had escaped police searches, or released by windup gramophones that had been patched up and greased during the summer, and that, despite the efforts of our red technicians, rarely succeeded at remaining operational for more than half a day. Revolutionary music, Komsomol choruses, and Soviet tangos from the third decade of the twentieth century, so indispensable to our culture, provided round-the-clock accompaniment to demonstration preparations. Tests and repetitions had fatal consequences for the mechanisms, and often, come the actual day of Bolcho Pride, they expelled grating hiccups instead of lively melodies, or remained mute. Nonetheless, there were enough surviving machines, and enough loudspeakers, to give ample triumph to the sonic ambiance of the event.

Granny Holgolde clearly felt younger around this time of year. The adults would bring it up in their conversations and banter, and she herself would recognize it, with a touch of mischief, claiming that the wind and scent of October had always quickened her pulse, regenerated her neurons, and kept her skin free from the blemishes of old age.

But, this year, things had taken a turn for the worse, and Bolcho Pride was a festival of violence and suffering.

You are burning. I go to you. In this moment, we are with you. We are all moving toward you. We are exchanging our last breaths.

Your memory trickles from your eyes.

My memories are yours.

2.

You are burning on the second floor of the Kam Yip Building. Everything is crackling around you. Drogman Baatar is dead. We are all moving toward you. We are exchanging our last breaths. My memories are yours.

You are burning on the second floor of the Kam Yip Building. Everything is crackling around you. Drogman Baatar is dead. I am moving toward you. In this moment, we are with you. We are all moving toward you. We are exchanging our last breaths.

Your memory trickles from your eyes.

My memories are yours.

You are burning on the second floor of the Kam Yip Building. Everything is crackling around you. Drogman Baatar is dead. Elli Zlank is burning too, somewhere on the ground floor. Maryama Adougaï is no longer screaming for help.

Fires have been a part of our daily lives since infancy. The camp's apartment buildings had faulty electrical installations. There was one short circuit after another. They were often benign, to no consequence other than outages and the stench of melting plastic, though sometimes they were more serious, and we had to quickly evacuate our homes, surrounded by shouts, smoke, and panic. There were also the bombs dropped from the sky by the enemy, always accompanied by immense flames and suffering.

That is why, even during periods of calm, we believed we were both subhumans and dwellers in ruins and fire.

I remember the books we used to read, the stories the adults used to tell us. Our culture went in many directions, but, in most cases, it reflected the reality of our routine: an egalitarian brotherhood desecrated by all, a panorama of ashes, barricades, imprisonment, a heavy sky, and from above, the fatal burst of flames.

I am moving toward you. In this moment, we are with you. We are all moving toward you. We are exchanging our last breaths.

Your memory trickles from your eyes.

My memories are yours.

You are burning on the second floor of the Kam Yip Building. Everything is crackling around you. Drogman Baatar is dead. Elli Zlank is burning too, somewhere on the ground floor. Maryama Adougaï is no longer screaming for help. She may no longer be alive.

You close your eyes, you mumble confused words, as if your body were already no longer your own, no longer responding to you, translating into your mouth a drunkard's miserable slurrings.

Fires have been a part of our daily lives since infancy. The camp's apartment buildings had faulty electrical installations. There was one short circuit after another. They were often benign, to no consequence other than outages and the stench of melting plastic, though sometimes they were more serious, and we had to quickly evacuate our homes, surrounded by shouts, smoke, and panic. There were also the bombs dropped from the sky by the enemy, always accompanied by immense flames and suffering.

That is why, even during periods of calm, we believed we were both subhumans and dwellers in ruins and fire.

I remember the books we used to read, the stories the adults used to tell us. Our culture went in many directions, but, in most cases, it reflected the reality of our routine. After journeying through oneiric lands, we would quickly return to the territories we had always known: an egalitarian brotherhood desecrated by all, a panorama of ashes, barricades, imprisonment, a heavy sky, and from above, the fatal burst of flames.

Let us take, for example, the fantastical narrations Granny Holgolde invented for us when she wasn't busy managing our concealment or planning the insurrectional tempests meant, in a few fiery days and nights, to set things right on Earth. Granny Holgolde loved to laugh, she loved the humor of disaster, and all her stories were nowhere near as mournful as our ordinary landscapes, though many of them were. I'm thinking in particular of the ones about our favorite heroines: the elephant Marta Ashkarot or Igriyana Gogshog, the old wandering killer, or even Bobby Potemkine, the sad loser. Nor am I forgetting the tales in which those half-human birds Granny Holgolde called strange cormorants appeared, the ones who knew how to live in fire, secrecy, and death. None of those stories were specifically meant for children, save for their educational function. It was a matter of not letting our sense of the magical be misled down too-ambivalent paths; it was also a matter of giving us role models to better face adversity, at least until our deaths. To know what to do when the time comes, know how to overcome our terror, know how to keep courage and strike down the enemy at all costs.

An image here of Granny Holgolde.

There. We are gathered, standing, sitting, around her. We are waiting for her to recount Marta Ashkarot's or Igriyana Gogshog's adventure, left unfinished from the week before. You are there too, Imayo Özbeg, with your chestnut locks hanging down the middle of your forehead, the rest of your hair disheveled, and your shining black eyes, a dreamer's eyes, usually fixed not on us, but on new horizons.

I had just turned seven when the adults around us started talking about a Bolcho Pride that would be like none other. We slyly repeated the bits of phrases we caught when they talked among themselves. As we understood it, the great demonstration would be even more euphoric than usual. Our astrologers had calculated that we were no more than one hundred years away from the beginning of the world revolution. Only one-hundred-times-three-hundred-sixty-five days now separated us from the irrepressible tide of the humble, of their definitive surge into the annals of history. One-hundred-times-twelve months of nothing until, in all the cities, on all the continents, the camps would empty, the egalitarian insurrection would fly from victory to victory, the poor would take destiny into their own hands: thus had our red legends predicted since the dawn of time. One round century, and then things would improve for the global population. There would be no more waiting forever.

"Things are taking a good turn," Granny Holgolde assured us.

We politely stepped aside to avoid her wolf-like breath and sputters.

"They're on track to succeed," she claimed.

She was chewing on dried ewe's cheese mixed with strips of smoked meat, a typical snack of that era, enjoyed mainly during the autumnal celebrations. Our minor retreat did not offend her. She was hard set in her ways, extolling an iron hierarchy in the Party and respect for one's elders, but with us, her great-grandchildren, she forgave everything.

Granny Holgolde was unbelievably old; her legs no longer carried her and her body had decided to shrivel up over the past sixty years, but she had kept her great big head from her younger years, and, even if her chewing reminded us of a cow's rumination, we didn't feel so uncomfortable that we wouldn't rub against her when we were brought to greet her.

"It'll come very quickly now," she rejoiced.

Her small, milky gray eyes sparkled with political satisfaction, revolutionary zeal, and her love for good food.

"Prepare yourselves, little ones," she said heatedly. "Prepare yourselves, it's coming fast, as if tomorrow!"

Other images still.

I go to you. In this moment, we are with you. We are all moving toward you. We are exchanging our last breaths.

Your memory trickles from your eyes.

My memories are yours.

3.

Other images still.

I go to you. In this moment, we are with you. We are all moving toward you. We are exchanging our last breaths.

Your memory trickles from your eyes.

My memories are yours.

Other images still.

Granny Holgolde had the hiccups. She was drinking something. A second earlier, her stomach had sent up to her tongue a bit of ewe's milk and pemmican, and now she was swallowing it again. She pushed her glasses, which had slid down, back on her nose, then she gulped down several more mouthfuls. The drink had whitened the rim of her mouth and formed a small pearl on the mustache adorning her upper lip. She calmly emptied her glass and placed it next to the armchair that served as her throne twenty-four hours a day. She never slept, in the hope of witnessing, no matter the time, the awakening of the world revolution, the widespread conflagration, and the advent of proletarian brotherhood. The glass clinked on the bedside table and, since it was too close to the edge and threatened to fall, Aunt Boyol hurriedly stuck out her hand and pushed it back.

No one else had budged, particularly among the children. Granny Holgolde had interrupted her tale to quench her thirst, but she had not declared that she would continue the story later. She had simply taken a short break, and at a critical moment, too, when the elephant Marta Ashkarot smelled before her the presence of the void and decided not to take a single step more until the light of day had returned. Like the elephant, we had just been plodding slowly through the darkness, watching out for everything, the scents of the equatorial forest, the sounds and silences of the night, the quivering of leaves in the undergrowth. The parenthesis of the ewe's milk was closed. Granny Holgolde wiped her lips with the back of her hand. We were about to sniff once again before us, with our trunk, in order to discover whether the ravine at our feet was deep or shallow.

About once a month, the grandmothers and aunts who had us in their charge brought us to Granny Holgolde. For security reasons, she often changed residences, but she always carried with her her throne and her smell of curdled dairy, her smells of campfire, mushrooms, and handmade bombs. We were gathered before her, in a semicircle, fifteen or so little boys and girls, our eyes glued to her. Granny Holgolde spoke from a poorly lit alcove, in a corner of the main room of the house that had been hers for the past half year and that she called the sovkhoz, because the windows looked out onto an abandoned plot of land where two geese and a black dog often roamed. The real animals interested us, but Marta Ashkarot, the elephant, took priority. She existed within Granny Holgolde's tale, within Granny Holgolde's head and mouth, and we watched nothing else.

In the large room also stood the soldier Daravidias and the soldier Brudmann, as well as the inevitable sanitary inspector, who was in uniform and took notes on the state of the premises, the identities of those present, and the tenor of their words. The sanitary inspector's name was certainly inscribed on the tag pinned to her breast pocket, but we despised her too much to ever dream of trying to distinguish her from the other camp guards with whom fate had forced us to live. No one looked at her, no one was interested in her movements, she remained a nameless enemy, a member of one of the camp's obscure repressive institutions, and, though every one of us fantasized about opportunities and ways to kill her, we refused her the right to exist clearly in our thoughts. I have no desire to alter her status now. She moved among us while scribbling who knows what information in her official notebook, but she was not part of the room. She was not part of the room, and so enough about her.

From time to time, the soldier Daravidias and the soldier Brudmann glanced toward the window. This was a period when the majority of the members of the Werschwell Fraction had left for the front, and when pogromist raids were becoming increasingly rare, doubtlessly because, in order to reach us, they had to break through too many barricades. Since our childhood, if one excludes the bombardments, spontaneous fires, and nocturnal arrests, the camp had been a safe place for us. Nonetheless, the soldier Daravidias and the soldier Brudmann assumed their responsibilities and kept watch outside. They were at the ready to organize our defense, and I know that the presence of the sanitary inspector reassured them, since in the case of the enemy's unforeseen intervention, they would have immediately taken her hostage.

On the other side of the window, in the vague plot of land and even beyond the fence crowned by barbed wire, nothing was happening. The geese, plump and ridiculous, were milling about between two clumps of burdock. The dog was sleeping.

"And then, my little ones," Granny Holgolde continued, "the elephant grew wary. It was better to wait for dawn, the light's return, rather than rush blindly over a precipice. It was better to take two steps back than one step forward."

Granny Holgolde furrowed her already very wrinkled face and cleared her throat, like she always did when she was going to make an important remark. We knew this signal well. We concentrated even harder.

"You know, my little ones, sometimes you have to step back a little or tread water while waiting for the darkness to pass. What is essential is not to lose sight of advancing, of moving forward at all costs, and of not giving up. Even if something blinds us, we can't lose sight of that. You must always remember, never give up."

Suddenly, Granny Holgolde became animated. Her head was once more filled with grandiose objectives, the terminal defeat of misfortune, the triumphal dance of the proletariat all across the planet, peace and equality between primates, undermen, and human or semi-human species. Her eyes were sparkling. She scratched her stomach through her yellowish cotton blouse.

At the same time as the elephant's thoughts, some of these grandiose objectives filtered into us, inevitably.

The sanitary inspector took notes.

We were speechless.

"Yes, my gentle ones, all that matters is knowing that we will never give up, and that, even when we get there, well established, in the comfort of the revolution, we must continue moving forward without stopping!"

We were all wide-eyed, drinking in the storyteller's words. I am going to try to remember everyone who was there.

Imayo Özbeg, with his strand of hair stuck to his forehead.

My cousins Bouïna Yogideth, Maryama Adougaï, Wulva Kanaan, Lilni and Doumda Daliko, Rishma Bakitron, Rita Mirvrakis, Adoulia Brougz.

Little Drogman Baatar, chubby but fretful, with very dark hair.

The Ming twins.

Laura Gheen, who, despite her age of seven, still had not spoken a word, but who, that aside, wasn't slow at all.

Elli Zlank, the worst dressed of us all.

The eldest of the group, Aliya Meteliyan, who had let most of the boys and girls inspect her crotch, admiring on her invitation the hairs that had begun to appear on her pubis.

And, to finish the list, my little brother and me.

At that moment, a bullet fired from who knows where shattered the window to our right, the window looking out onto the vague terrain. As vigilant as the soldier Daravidias and the soldier Brudmann were, they couldn't prevent the unpredictable shots from snipers. The bullet whizzed over our heads and landed somewhere inside the sanitary inspector, between her notebook and her neck.

The soldier Daravidias posted himself near the window while the grandmothers and aunts made us get on all fours and huddle together against the least exposed wall. Outside, we heard the sound of running, a frantic cackling, then a second shot. The dog was barking.

The soldier Brudmann crouched over the inspector, who was lying on the floor. He offered to examine her wound, but she rebuked him violently, as if she suspected him of wanting to take advantage of the situation to ogle her chest or strangle her.

"It's nothing," the soldier Daravidias said. "It's just a goose hunter who missed his target."

"We'll take care of you," the soldier Brudmann said to the sanitary inspector. "It's nothing, it was just a goose hunter."

Granny Holgolde shrugged her shoulders.

"Leave her alone," she advised. "We have nothing to do with her."

The inspector was struggling. She had begun to bleed and moan, but Granny Holgolde continued to forbid the soldier Brudmann from touching her.

"She took the bullet not far from her heart," Brudmann diagnosed and stood. "She's not going to make it. Someone'll have to either finish her off or take her to the hospital."

The inspector started screaming something unintelligible. Brudmann was staring down at her, without sympathy. The soldier Daravidias joined him.

"Don't worry," he said to the woman. "It's going to pass. It wasn't meant for you."

"Leave her alone," Granny Holgolde repeated. "Let her be. We have nothing to do with her, geese or not."

We, the little ones, witnessed the scene while lamenting the consequences of the rifle: we would not know, for a long time, how Marta Ashkarot would cross the chasm that had opened in front of her.

Distant images.

I go to you. In this moment, we are with you. We are all moving toward you. We are exchanging our last breaths.

Your memory trickles from your eyes.

My memories are yours.

4.

Your memory trickles from your eyes.

Other scenes. Other sequences still that project themselves disorderedly onto the screens of our memory. Our childhood, our adolescence, then this part of time among the adults, this final journey that is ending poorly. You are burning. My memories are blending with those of my already dead or dying comrades. I go to you. My memories are yours. The images are deteriorated, they are lost, they are distant. Some contain sounds and smells, others do not. Under the influence of cinema, in unconscious homage to those screenings in unventilated rooms, in hidden cellars, some have subtitles, like in foreign films. Other images are in black and white, or sepia, though they are recent ones.

They are very recent, even. But their emotion is too strong and they appear as events from thirty or forty years ago, though it was actually hours, not years. Thirty or forty hours have passed, or perhaps fewer. These images belong to the immediate present, though they are already yellowed from the fumes, deformed by the night, by destruction, by dreams. Already, a number of men and women who appear in them breathe no more. Already, they no longer have a body, now living through the first hallucinations of death, imagining that they have been transformed into strange cormorants, or that they are groping around with disgust in the sooty halls where they were absorbed once deceased. Already they are walking in shadows, their only consolation a glass of ewe's milk and a few crumbs of pemmican that they must ration if they want to hold out for forty-nine days.

I go to you. In this moment, we are with you. We are all moving toward you, toward all of you. We are exchanging our last breaths. Beside Imayo Özbeg, Elli Zlank, and Drogman Baatar are those who accompanied them in the disastrous attack on the Kam Yip

Building and who also find themselves trapped by the flames: Maryama Adougaï, Ouassila Albachvili, Dariana Freek, Loula Maldarivian, Taïa "Chicha" Torff. All in this moment have stopped fighting, they are stretching their hands toward the shadows, finding nothing, understanding nothing. They walk with difficulty, having lost their bodies, their ability to judge and decide, their sense of reality, going into the greatest possible solitude, obliterated, having lost everything. The memories of these final days are there, more in me than in you. Landscapes both interior and exterior have been ruined by bister soot, cooked flesh, and death. We are all moving toward Imayo Özbeg, we are all moving toward you with these memories, these incredibly recent memories preceding our last, catastrophic Bolcho Pride.

It was thirty or forty hours ago, or perhaps fewer.

The night. There is a light rain. As a cost-saving measure, and to impede the preparations of the imminent Pride, the camp's administration has plunged the Negrini Bloc, along with neighboring districts, into darkness. The camp reeks of the damp, light-deprived night, it reeks of soaked hovels, dilapidated clothes, faces, hair, and dreams. Eleonor Ouzbachi Street is dark. Margyar Schrag Avenue is dark.

Kordobane Street is dark, too. But something is blazing three hundred meters away, at its intersection with Kwam Kok Boulevard.

Suddenly you can see Granny Holgolde, hurrying toward the fire. She is dressed in dark rags, with a jabot made of faded white lace that ruffled against her large chest, and a skirt that resembles a petticoat. She is jogging. You can hear her ragged breaths. Although in our youth, she was confined to her nonagenarian's armchair, she has never stopped growing younger, and, on that night, two days ago, she possesses the form of a widow of seventy years, or even fewer, held back by no medical complications. She is brandishing a hatchet to attack the flame-locked doors, and, as she runs, she's striking every balustrade and iron slab she passes. She is shouting.

She wants to sound the alarm and wake every sleeping activist, sympathizer, Party member, and fellow traveler.

The more time passes, the more the light of the flames reflects off the drizzle-soaked street and Granny Holgolde's hard physiognomy, deformed by her hatred for the fire and the emotion of the current disaster. What is burning, now very close, fifty meters away, is the place where we store our belongings, the masks, flags, and cardboard statues that show off the glory of the Negrini Bloc during Bolcho Pride.

A few silhouettes come and go. Some stand frozen before the spectacle.

Bolshevik Pride days have always been divided into three categories: extremely successful, somewhat successful, and disappointing. This one promises to be one of the worst yet. In the night, on Kordobane Street, we already know that it will have to be classified separately—not disappointing, but catastrophic.

Granny Holgolde throws herself onto the building's entrance and swings her hatchet into it. Passersby try to pull her away. There is no way to save whatever remains inside. The flames whirl and roar louder and louder. The heat rises from moment to moment. The passersby seize Granny Holgolde by the waist, by the shoulders, they shout at her that no one is trapped in there, that only objects will be destroyed, that she has to get away from the fire. Imayo Özbeg struggles to take the hatchet from her hands. She resists. She fights back. The action is confused. From a distance, since everyone is yelling and moving about, the scene looks like a group of quarreling drunks. I approach in turn. Granny Holgolde is dripping with sweat, her glistening skin like crimson copper. She reluctantly lets go of her weapon. Something explodes upstairs. Grit and embers scatter above us, raining down. It's time to leave.

Granny Holgolde catches her breath. In the light of the flames, she resembles an old goddess made of terracotta. For some reason, Taïa "Chicha" Torff carefully wipes Granny Holgolde's face, then ties a grayish bandana around her head. Granny Holgolde thanks her as she picks up her hatchet, which she is now holding, letting it swing against her leg.

"We have to find out who's done this," Granny Holgolde mutters. "They have to be punished."

We all made vague signs of agreement. Needless to say, when we can get our hands on a wrongdoer, we don't get in the way of making them pay for their crimes. But, here, everything points to there not being enough time to carry out an investigation before Bolcho Pride. The guilty party might be a saboteur, or someone careless who tossed a cigarette butt behind them without putting it out, or, most likely, the guilty party is bad luck. The electrical wiring caused a short circuit. There is no one to punish.

"If I find him," Granny Holgolde said, "I won't hesitate to take care of him myself. I've got everything I need right here to crack open his skull."

Opposite us, the warehouse burns.

On Kwam Kok Boulevard, half a dozen comrades rush back and forth with buckets and a cistern on a lurching cart. Nothing will be saved.

We think again of what the Chinese in the Margyar Schrag Barracks said to us. According to them, we have entered a Water Goat year, and their annals attest that this is an astrological combination unfavorable to humans and subhumans, as well as to bolshevism in general. We see once more Granny Holgolde shrug her shoulders and treat them like birds of ill omen, and declaring, as she laughs with them, that she only pays attention to prophecies when they announce the coming collapse of capitalism.

Whatever it is, opposite us, the warehouse burns.

The days of Bolshevik Pride have always unfurled in comparable scenarios and, in order for our memory to tell them apart, we attribute to them a grade of satisfaction: magnificent, not too bad, or terrible. This one is already in a class of its own, below all others. It starts with a calamity.

Once again, something explodes upstairs. A torrential braid, sometimes orange, sometimes black, writhes through a window.

Granny Holgolde shakes her hatchet and trembles with rage.

"Bring that son of a bitch to me," she demands.

Then it is morning. An infamous dawn over Kordobane Street. Everything has been reduced to ash.

So as not to have a lackluster parade, we decide to hastily rebuild everything that has been destroyed. Only one day remains before the start of the festival and we don't have a minute to spare.

We withdraw into another empty space, Dolmar Dong Crossing. Granny Holgolde sits in a corner and directs the operations, but, despite her iron will and excellent health, she feels the repercussions of spending the entire night awake and, from time to time, begins to nod off. Between two thundering instructions, her eyes close. We then hear her snoring like an old woman and begin to think that she hasn't really rejuvenated as much as she tells us. She wakes without warning and immediately exhorts us to work faster. It's obvious that we shouldn't inform her of her mid-sentence nap. The bandana Chicha tied around her forehead slides more and more often over her eyelids. With her wizened hands wringing on top of her tattered black skirt, she looks more like a mental patient than a director of the Party's secret structures.

Under this slightly cantankerous surveillance, we try to attend to the most pressing matters. The day should have been dedicated to the uprooting and defacing of signs posted by the administration, threatening proclamations outlawing our parade, outlawing any gathering of demonstrators, outlawing costumes and slogans, authorizing only a handful of cotton candy stands and book stalls, along with a list of forbidden publications. Instead of roaming the streets with containers of tar to render all of this prose illegible, we are cutting up scraps of fabric to serve as flags. All we have at our disposal are old shirts and rags. We have nothing to dye them red. Our reserves of andrinople and vermilion paint are still smoking at the intersection of Kordobane Street and Kwam Kok Boulevard. Drogman Baatar is drawing raised fists, stars, submachine guns, and intertwined hammers and sickles on pieces of cloth, his paintbrush dripping with oil. Elli Zlank has requisitioned the firefighters' useless cart, removed the cistern, and is nailing together hardboard silhouettes meant to replace the people's commissars who were carbonized just a few hours ago. The silhouettes are all the same. Granny Holgolde tasks me and Maryama Adougaï with personalizing them. She insists that we place signs around their necks bearing their names. It's a bad idea, but she insists. I think it brings to mind the infamous and defamatory signs the Ybürs have to wear on their backs when they leave the camp for work or to wander around the city, in the extraordinary case that they've survived extermination.

"With that around their necks, they'll look like punching bags," I say.

"You have a twisted mind, my child," Granny Holgolde reproaches.

"My parents wore signs like that before they were shot," Imayo Özbeg says.

Granny Holgolde's face darkens once more.

"With their names hanging from their necks, they'd look like undesirable individuals," Drogman Baatar suddenly chimes in, standing next to us with a can of motor oil. "Undesirable individuals denounced before the masses, during the First Chinese Cultural Revolution. They're just missing a pointed hat."

"To me," Maryama Adougaï interrupts, "the leaders' silhouettes look like training targets at a shooting range."

"You children are full of nonsense today," Granny Holgolde protests.

We are all tired. The flags are incredibly ugly. Our plywood helmsmen don't look like their prestigious models, they look like nothing, they look like undesirable individuals, like counterrevolutionaries of the ninth stinking category, like targets. The firefighters' cart brings to mind a wagon for the condemned. When we march to express our pride, the Negrini Bloc's vanguard will seem like a carnival of exhausted mendicants, emerging from a world without color or form, emerging from a strange mass grave, already dead but electrified by a posthumous will to forget nothing, never to give up for any reason, to renounce none of the virtues buried with them long ago. And devoutly conveying vague, wooden, forgotten, unspeakable gods, transporting them to who knows what dismal execution site, still celebrating them despite their obvious defeat and impossible persistence.

Then someone enters with an accordion and begins to play waltzes from the Second Soviet Union, and Granny Holgolde rises, chooses Elli Zlank as a dance partner, and twirls impeccably, though with a certain diligence, which adds an unnatural element to her elegance.

The image of Granny Holgolde, several hours before the worst of our Bolshevik Prides, turning in rhythm inside an old truck depot, surrounded by poorly made flags, drooping plywood, oil stains. One of the very last images.

Distant images. Farther and farther away. Closer and closer.

I go to you. In this moment, we are with you. We are all moving toward you. We are exchanging our last breaths.

Your memory trickles from your eyes.

My memories are yours.

It was a basic elephant trap. A wire stretched across the trail, right where pachyderms were likely to tread; two stakes to hold the wire in place, which only a very large animal would have the strength to unearth; a mechanism to shoot off a cluster of firecrackers; and the firecrackers themselves. Simply tripping over it would blow everything up in three seconds flat. The humans who had created it didn't want to injure or kill, and in any case, they didn't have the technology to whip up a lethal weapon, but they were counting on the frightful suddenness of the detonations to awake in the animal a feeling of terror. The elephant could only quickly turn back around and flee, panic-stricken, unable to comprehend the din in the darkness a few steps ahead of it. It would remember a lasting fear, and would never come back. Such was the function of the trap. Such was its philosophy.

Marta Ashkarot walked a few meters forward without touching the wire that barred the route. She observed the firing mechanism for a moment and then defused it with the tip of her trunk. Then she picked up a firecracker and began to chew on it pensively. Several years before, she had discovered that she enjoyed the taste of potassium nitrate. She never overindulged, but, when the opportunity presented itself, she didn't deny herself the small pleasure. Even the wrapping had a candy-like appeal: the spoonful of plaster, the cardboard tube. Even the by-products had an agreeable flavor: the charcoal, the sulfur.

Oh yes, she thought. Oh yes, indeed. I'm quite the foodie, aren't I?

The veil of bamboo was thick enough to conceal her, and she moved with suppleness, without crunching the fallen leaves all around her. If, in spite of the late hour, anyone were keeping watch, they wouldn't have been able to detect her presence. She approached the vegetation's edge and stopped to observe what lay beyond.

Before her feet were cultivated fields, sweet potato plantations, and the village's territory.

It was night, a moonless night. Beyond the fields, a dozen shacks were lined up around a rectangle of beaten earth, which must have had the pretension of being a street, the main and only street in the settlement. A single light was on. It shone above a hovel even smaller than the others, though less dilapidated.

An administrative building, Marta Ashkarot deduced.

Administration! the elephant thought. The hominids' last pride before their return to the primitive horde or their pure and simple disappearance. It's what separates them from animals. One last collective affirmation, as important for them as their subsistence agriculture and firecrackers.

The lamp illuminated an overhang. Still unmoving in her plant-covered hiding spot, Marta Ashkarot concentrated her gaze. At the risk of being blinded, she stared at the light and its surrounding environs. She wanted to figure out what sort of institution was hosted behind those planks. Sometimes, humans or assimilees continued to practice the art of writing, scribbling on walls the handful of official terms they had retained. If that's an institution, they may have slathered its name in paint somewhere, the elephant thought.

Several medium-sized, rather active spiders could be tallied in the light; they were busy wrapping freshly caught butterflies in silk. But there was no visible inscription that indicated the nature of the administration or its hours of operation. In contrast to the night, the light fixture was a form of optical violence. Marta Ashkarot averted her eyes and squeezed shut her eyelids five or six times to fill them with tears and dispel the imprint of the incandescent filaments. She waited for her optic nerve to stop sending her messages in burn marks and thunderbolts.

She waited for a long minute.

She reflected.

Spiders eating butterflies. A lamp lit in front of an office, on the village's main street. Hominids sleeping in their filthy huts.

Nothing out of the ordinary, really, she thought.

The stars in her ocular globes had finally stopped dancing.

She shook her immense ears. The bamboo leaves rustled against her skin. The powerful stalks hung like springs over her neck, her flanks.

Alright, I'm going over there, she decided.

She pushed through the bamboo stalks without breaking them and exited the thicket. Now she was out in the open. The ground was dusty, and after a damp, watered layer, became hard. Her feet left practically no prints in the soil.

She crossed the vegetable patches, stepped onto the street, and stopped before the administrative shack and its lightbulb. The building did not have an ironclad solidity. It was obvious that a pachyderm attempting to squeeze inside would distort the entire frame.

The man working the desk had heard a noise and must have feared that his guest was taking the initiative to enter, for suddenly he clicked a latch, put a rudimentary wooden sign on himself, and appeared at the threshold, his hand raised above his forehead, more to protect himself from the light of the lamp than to salute any sort of greeting.

"Would you mind if I turned that off?" he asked.

"No," the elephant said.

They remained there for several moments, saying nothing. The man had just switched off the electricity and there they were, face to face, waiting for their filament-blinded retinal tissues to reconstruct themselves.

"It's protocol," the man finally said. "It's bad for your eyes, and keeps you from seeing in the dark, but those are the orders."

"Ah," the elephant said.

"Do you remember the First Soviet Union? Right at the start, someone said that if the Soviets wanted to achieve communism, they first needed more electricity. He was a short bald man. His name escapes me."

"I vaguely recall," Marta Ashkarot reflected. "Soviets, more electricity, yes. But I no longer remember whether it was to achieve communism or socialism. That was seven or eight centuries ago, at any rate."

She swayed back and forth, and, when her head approached the awning, she felt the heat of the bulb, its filament taking some time to cool, and smelled the scent of the butterflies dissolving from the gastric juices that the spiders had injected into them.

The man was not afraid of her and stood a meter away, calmly, without gesticulating, quite the opposite of how peasants act in the presence of pachyderms.

"At any case, in the long run, we got there," the man said. "That bald Russian was right."

Marta Ashkarot silently agreed. Then, with her trunk, she gestured toward the shack that, now no longer artificially illuminated, was much more visible.

"Is that the village soviet?" she asked.

"It was, yes," the man explained. "The village soviet. But, in the surrounding areas, there was a decline in population, so we regrouped. Now, it's more of a regional soviet. Interregional even, since there's not much else around anymore."

"Hmmm! Interregional!" the elephant exclaimed in admiration.

"Well, yes," the man said.

He puffed out his chest, as if he felt invested with a titanic responsibility, and Marta Ashkarot noticed that he was wobbling slightly. There was no smell of alcohol on his breath. Perhaps he had succumbed to the giddiness of success.

Their dialogue paused. Around them, the village was sleeping.

Four houses were inhabited, maybe five. At the center was a medium-sized agglomeration, on which circumstances had bestowed the status of capital. In the context of the population's rarefaction and even extinction, the soviet administered a nearly continental territory.

"That does mean though," the man continued, "that with this lamp and this soviet, communism presides over an immense part of the world."

"I don't know about communism," Marta Ashkarot rectified. "Maybe just its preparatory phase. Maybe just socialism."

The man continued puffing out his chest.

"Hardly matters," he said.

"Yes," the elephant conceded. "No reason to quibble over words."

"Of course not," the man said. "Words don't matter. What matters is that it's been established. And this time, it's here to stay."

Granny Holgolde's Tale: The Paper

Marta Ashkarot shoved her shoulder one last time against the dark wall. The bricks came loose, just a few at first, as if the wall were accepting its wounds with regret, then, suddenly, the whole structure collapsed. The hole was enormous and, once the fracas had died down, Marta Ashkarot stepped over the rubble. She crossed through the dust and entered into her new home. Her old abode instantly faded into a nebulous bad memory. Thus the elephant had gone, from home to home, for several centuries, without asking too many questions about the inevitable or the end. Everything had begun inside a dream, and the system functioned without any glitches: she led a normal life, associated with one home or another, and then, when the time of her personal extinction approached, a force pushed her toward a change in habitation, often either in a rather strange manner or while she slept. She then found herself in another existence, in the next home, and she started all over again, just like everyone else.

She started all over again, certainly, just like everyone else. But, even though she hadn't asked fate for it, she benefited from favorable treatment. Whenever she changed existences, she only had to go through the phases of rebirth and the choice of wombs, and not through the phases of childhood or adolescence, with their countless atrocious episodes of training, apprenticeship, and indoctrination. She passed directly from one adulthood to the next. The process came about after her first death, and, ever since, it hadn't changed. That said, the transition was not without fear or pain. Often, Marta Ashkarot felt that she was brushing against a barrier that just barely separated her from death or something comparable, just as horrible, or even more horrible than death. And sometimes she was also convinced that the home she had left would be replaced with nothing. At the very worst moment, when she was counting her respirations in order to stave off her final breath, something would whisper into her mind that her consciousness was going to cease to exist, that she herself had arrived at the end of the road, and that, now, the agony of death would be revealed to her, followed by complete darkness. But fortunately, up to this point, reality had always refuted her apprehensions. And when, once more established someplace new, she thought back on the anguishes she had suffered, she chalked them up to a natural phenomenon from which she was not the only creature to suffer, and that, to the contrary, must torment many individuals, such as animals that shed their skin, or that hide themselves in borrowed shells, or especially the ones that slumber inside cocoons in order to soften themselves into a foul pulp, so as to be reconstituted in an ephemeral form, intended for egg-laying and death. It's true that the comparison had no scientific basis. Well no, she reflected, elephants don't wander through saltwater in search of a better-fitting shell. Nor do they sleep in their own silk and dream of waking up with wings. At any rate, I've never been particularly envious of wings, she concluded.

The mechanism for her survival had been first set in motion within a dream, she remembered, but that explained nothing, since, ever since that time, she hadn't resided in any oneiric world at all. She had noted no difference in her existence from before. Something had simply changed for her in the succession of physiological periods and, in brief, she never reached old age. Whenever decline reared its head, she would be taken by an irrepressible will to action. All the cells in her body would whisper to her that the time had come to move on. And then she would leave her home, travel down a dark alley when she was in an urban environment, or through a thicket of tall grass if in the countryside, and she would trot straight ahead, guided more by instinct than rational calculations, until she pushed her way into a newfound home. That's how it went. The installation within four walls took some time to materialize, the walk had its crepuscular and arduous parts, but, in most cases, it took no longer than forty-nine days.

Often, the place where Marta Ashkarot was obliged to start her existence anew differed little from the one she had just left behind. But it also happened to entail a radical change in scenery, social circle, and culture. So Marta Ashkarot adapted, all while making sure to keep her biological, ideological, and intellectual markers intact. When the windows of her new home opened onto a world governed by counterrevolution, extermination, or religious wars, she joined resistance organizations—if they still existed—and waited for what was to come. Neither stoically, nor heroically, nor miserably, she waited for what was to come. And it always came, no matter what. It was just a matter of preparing herself and knowing how to react at just the right moment.

Sometimes, Marta Ashkarot's journey through one existence would not last long. She would have just enough time to enter a new place and get her bearings when suddenly she'd find herself sliding down a new corridor to leave once more. These short experiences could generally be explained by the fact that she had burst forth into one region or another on the globe where the genocidal atmosphere was unbreathable. In places like those, Marta Ashkarot figured among the potential victims and, after a very brief period, she would be caught by the killers. But there were also chains of circumstances that could not be linked to the ethno-political abominations of hominids, and which were simply unlucky. For example, she might be confronted with unforeseen climatic catastrophes or epidemics. She had thus traversed the multiplication of the seas of bitumen, the bird flu pandemic, and even a gas explosion at 9 Brim Akaouliev Street, where she was living in the ground-floor apartment as a shaman. She always referred to her march into a new existence as a move—an adequate term, in one sense, since it certainly consisted of translating from one home to another, but also, in another sense, an inadequate term, for she passed from one place to another without bringing along any bags or personal effects, completely nude.

And, this time, the journey was undertaken with complication and slowness, even though, for the last step, she only had to shove through a tiny brick partition. The march that had preceded this liberatory moment had been long and tedious. She had met with falls, darkness, days of extreme solitude inside extremely dirty labyrinths. For weeks, without food or water or any way to counter the pressure of the intense blackness on her body and mind, Marta Ashkarot had progressed from cellar to cellar, from tunnel to tunnel. The interminable process had been nothing but a series of obstacles. At every instant she had to knock down walls by pressing down on them with all her weight. She ultimately imagined that she was moving through an old prison of phenomenally vast dimensions, or an abandoned military factory, or a monastery whose cells were all firmly shut. She stuck to the north-north-eastward course she had chosen at the start, without thinking about it too much, and which she had maintained despite the difficulties, so as not to get turned around. She would break her way into a new room, wait for the suffocating dance of dust to end, then almost immediately begin to feel around for the next demolition.

Seven long, monotonous weeks were thus spent smashing piles of cinderblocks, splitting plywood, or exploding brick barriers. The situation had worsened in the final fifteen days, as there had been a bloom of miasmatic plagues. The air had become nothing but a decoction of pathogenic horrors. Marta Ashkarot's lungs refused to absorb such a toxic mixture, and the elephant finished her dark trek in apnea.

As she destroyed the final wall, Marta Ashkarot still had no idea that she was reaching the end of her grueling journey. The bricks scattered and she was suddenly bathed in light. Real air filled her mouth, reached her trachea, and beat a path to her lungs. Just like in the jungle and in her dreams, she lifted her trunk, held it between the bumps on her head, and began to trumpet. An intense satisfaction enveloped her. She now understood that her move was over. She opened her eyes wide.

She opened her eyes wide. Then she stepped over the rubble and entered her new home.

She wasn't alone. Oh I see, she thought, this place is already occupied.

She was in a large meeting room, with a long table in its center that resembled those imposing pieces of furniture in public libraries where each seat is marked by a number and an individual lamp. There were no numbers here, but, as outside it was already night, the lamps illuminated from below twenty or so people sitting with sheets of paper and pencils. Everyone had the appearance and clothes of functionaries, or perhaps worker and peasant syndicalists. Men, women. Many of them turned to look at Marta Ashkarot.

"We were waiting for you to come back," one of them said.

Marta Ashkarot glanced over her shoulder. Contrary to what was still in her immediate memory, the walls hadn't suffered from her entrance into the room. No heap of debris exhaled dust behind her. In reality, the second before, she had just come through a quite ordinary door. A windowed door. She had come through it without breaking anything and she had calmly closed it behind her. On the glass was attached a sign extolling the virtues of the union between proletarians, soldiers, and farmers, and, just above that, screwed into the wood, there was an enameled metal plaque indicating that on the other side were the women's restrooms.

Adapt, Marta Ashkarot thought.

Above all, don't lose your cool. Adapt and integrate.

She faced the assembly and quickly analyzed the group. Those present hadn't dressed in finery for the meeting, but they had clearly made an effort not to come in work clothes or overalls. Several of them were resting their strong laborer's hands on the table, on the duplicated sheets of paper detailing the day's agenda, and which were all still free of any sort of scribble.

Marta Ashkarot took note of these hands, the damaged nails and fingers highlighted by the individual lamps, then she cast her gaze around the vast room, with its excess chairs stacked in one corner, its large windows that opened onto a night poorly combated by urban illumination, its metal cabinets, its decorations consisting mainly of tourist advertisements and political posters. Then she sat down. There was a free chair to the right of the meeting's president.

"So," he said softly, "when you go to the bathroom, you take your time."

"Was there a problem?" the woman sitting next to her asked.

"There wasn't any paper," Marta Ashkarot explained. "I had to use the agenda."

"To clean yourself?"

"Yes, of course. To clean myself."

The four or five people who had heard Marta Ashkarot's explanation fidgeted and grimaced. They expressed their indignation by widening their eyes, but it was difficult to tell whether this indignation was pretend or real. After this demonstration of shock—the recipients of which being both Marta Ashkarot and the general assembly—they pivoted toward the president of the meeting. They were waiting for a reaction on his part. In the past, wiping oneself with an official document guaranteed a trip to the reeducation camp, or, in certain years, the platoon. Times had changed, but still.

"Well what," Marta Ashkarot continued. "It wasn't a formal communication from the Central Committee. It was nothing. Just some local matters. The schedule for the next meeting, repairing public enclosures, donations for the elderly."

The president cleared his throat, but said nothing. The appropriate words did not come to his lips.

"You could have used something else," the woman sitting next to Marta Ashkarot muttered.

"What, something else?" the elephant protested. "No, I couldn't have. And besides, times have changed."

There was a silence. She noticed that the entire room avoided meeting her gaze. Her neighbor had reddened and was preoccupying herself with a theatrical examination of the document in front of her. The president's face was stony. He cleared his throat once again.

Perhaps I've made a mistake in my assessment, Marta Ashkarot thought. This is going to be difficult to fix.

Now, opposite her, she noticed a delegate who was examining her with a grimace of disgust, the kind reserved for a traitor or an enemy. He was about to intervene.

Perhaps times haven't changed much, after all.

Liars' Bridge

When she went to fetch water, Maryama Adougaï had to pass
through Alley Number Eleven, cross over the old train track, and
head down Leel Fourmanova Street. She then came once again to
the train track, which she crossed anew, but this time by passing
below, as she had to set foot inside a small, lightless tunnel with
grimy walls, neither very tall nor very wide. Since time immemorial,
this place has been called Liars' Bridge. On the other side, the city
continued, but an immediate barrier blocked the way. You'd come
out of the tunnel and find yourself in a quite vast square, which
functioned as a sort of cul-de-sac. All the exits were closed off by
spiked blockades and barbed wire, stretched from one house to the
next, up to the second and sometimes even third floor, or knotted
into tangles to forbid access to the portion of train track looming
over the scenery. Beyond these titanic spiderwebs stretched Bloc
709: an urban sector emptied of its inhabitants, its streets full of
unsightly grasses, the smell of decay, bricked-up windows, façades
covered in black moss, crumbling barracks. The square, by contrast,
remained a lively place. In its center stood a deserted washhouse,
where we went to get water. From one of its walls jutted three
high-flow spigots. They were watched over by civil defense soldiers
whom camp authorities had entrusted with minor order-keeping
tasks. Since there was no schedule for using the washhouse, many of
us preferred to go at night, meaning that at even three or four in the
morning you could hear the sound of tanks being filled, the knocking of containers on the drain grate or the furrow's cement side, or
the voices of soldiers attempting to converse with water carriers.

Liars' Bridge had marked our childhoods in several ways, and
when I say our childhoods I obviously mean Maryama Adougaï's
as well. For some of us, she was our cousin, and for others, our
little sister. I remember, for example, the expeditions for water we
undertook in the company of the enormous Aunt Boyol, who at

the time, in the absence of our parents, who had left to fight or die elsewhere, had taken us under her wing. Officially, if the term could have any meaning in the Negrini Bloc, Aunt Boyol was our adoptive mother.

Aunt Boyol didn't allow us to treat passing under the bridge like any ordinary step on the road to the washhouse. She would assemble us before the dark opening and, to start, she would make us quiet down. We would stop our bickering and obediently park ourselves in front of her, like students with a schoolteacher. Once she had made sure that we were willing to listen to her, she would begin to tell us terrible things. We had already heard the story many times, but we always listened to it with a shiver of discovery. The passage beneath Liars' Bridge, she explained, was a test in which our fates hung in the balance. We could very easily lose our lives within: liars risked losing their heads halfway through.

Especially lying children, she'd clarify.

Aunt Boyol didn't ask us about any recent lies we might have been guilty of. She was content just to give us warning. She claimed that she had witnessed many times in the past the fatal punishment of boys and girls who had lied. They started to walk under the bridge like normal, when, suddenly, their head would go flying. They'd stagger back and forth, holding out their arms like the blind, swinging around wildly, then silently collapsed. That's how it happened, she continued, opening her eyes wide and miming the horrible scene.

Like many adults at the time, Aunt Boyol didn't resort to euphemisms, and so nothing softened the horror of her descriptions. We were thus entitled to the heads bouncing and rolling over the dirty ground, the bulging eyes whose lids would never close again, the gushing of blood from the space between shoulders. And, for good measure, the dead-meat sound of the body when it hit the ground. This was the expression she generally used when she wanted to impress us even more than usual. The dead-meat sound. Such tales put us in a state of intense dread, and through the years it produced an effect on our behavior. Since then, we've thought twice before lying, to be sure. But, above all, we'd learned to trick our minds into not remembering our lies. We had to wash out every inner stain and rebuild this falsely clean terrain with sincerity and innocence. Thanks to our mental gymnastics, the difficult truths and untruths that accompanied them were all blown away. This sort of powerful self-defense technique may have been exactly what Aunt Boyol was trying to teach us.

Once Aunt Boyol had finished her sermon, she'd make a gesture that meant the time for us to cross the threshold had come.

We would gather speed, suppress the butterflies in our stomachs, and dash, shouting, into the tunnel. It was only about fifteen meters long, but to us it seemed endless and infinitely dark. We were sure we were being chased by a flying meat cleaver, and we even sometimes very distinctly felt it graze the backs of our necks. I remember putting my hands behind my neck so the blade wouldn't nick my skin. Maryama Adougaï, who was five or six years old then, would let out ear-piercing shrieks that reverberated and magnified beneath the black vault. All around us, the walls stunk of the dampness, saltpeter, and rust of public urinals. Coming out the other side and touching the washhouse was our deliverance. For somewhat unclear reasons, which we never explored in depth, going back through the passage the other way presented no danger whatsoever, regardless of one's hypocritical fabulations, false declarations, or stories.

But Liars' Bridge wasn't just a lie detector or revealer of childish guilt. It was also the place where we witnessed our first deaths. In all likelihood the authorities chose the washhouse as a prime location for delivering their vision of the world and their messages because the need for water meant the people of the Negrini Bloc couldn't avoid going there. For example, when a new campaign for literacy, humanist hygiene, or moral reimplantation arose, we would often see the initial effects near the public spigots. The messages delivered by the authorities at those moments were easy to understand. They were composed in a universal language and practically always had the same content: magnanimity and even laxity toward those who complied, freedom of speech for those who followed the movement, extreme severity toward those who opposed the current campaign or persisted in advocating violent action and the murder of public officials.

Our first contact with corpses had shaken us, but, after a few difficult nights, the awfulness of our nightmares diminished, probably because those executed had lived in a barracks far from our own and weren't a part of our daily lives. We knew their names: Galbour Damdal and Drok Bamarbak. They had refused to be vaccinated, refused to go to the reeducation center, refused to salute the flag, and, on top of all that, they beat to death the humanitarian in charge of their case with a chair. Galbour Damdal's body was hung from the vault of Liars' Bridge, while Drok Bamarbak's was thrown onto the hedge of barbed wire that surrounded Bloc 709. The adults who came to fill their jerricans were obviously not allowed to take them down, and they gazed at the bodies while exhaling an endless series of sighs. That day, Aunt Boyol didn't give us a speech in front of the entrance to the tunnel, but, for my little sister Maryama Adougaï and myself, the fear of feeling a blade slice our necks was joined by the fear of our shoulders suddenly being touched by Galbour Damdal's cadaver, with its adult weight, its dampness, and its dead-meat sound.

Fifteen years later, and the camp authorities haven't changed at all, nor has Liars' Bridge and its urine-soaked stench, nor the organization of our daily existence, nor the journey for water, nor our collective ill will toward international charity programs, nor the persistence among the majority of us of ideologies glorifying armed vengeance and reprisals against those responsible for suffering. Aunt Boyol was still alive, as well. She had doubled in size, and, cloistered in her room, unable to move, was still growing. It seemed that she had said farewell to death and that her body had reacted to the prospect of life without end by swelling prodigiously. Interested in her case, a veterinary aid organization transferred her to a special laboratory, on the other side of the city, where we visited her once a month. She no longer recognized us. She spent her days humming old anarchist songs or muttering egalitarian sutras that explained how to rebuild the world upon new bases, starting with the absolute and definitive destruction of everything. It was enough to bring an ear to her mouth to understand that she had not lost her mind and that her program, though strongly colored by maximalism, had set quite reasonable limits for itself. Aunt Boyol wasn't deranged, but had simply, in the antiseptic chamber where she was held prisoner, withdrawn into herself, and was now waiting.

But let's get to the point.

Maryama Adougaï passed through Alley Number Eleven, crossed the old train track, and began to head down Leel Fourmanova Street. No one was accompanying her to the washhouse. She was now twenty years old. She had fashioned a wagon out of a plank outfitted with four wheels, on which she had placed two twelve-liter jerricans and a bucket with a lid. She was pulling the wagon by a rope. The wheels creaked as the cart noisily jostled over the uneven ground. It was three o'clock in the morning; the din resounded from one end of the deserted street to the other. The sky was dark, cloudy, lacking in heaviness since it was already autumn, when nocturnal storms become rare. The night was hot and still. In front of Liars' Bridge, Maryama Adougaï slowed and looked around. There was no other living soul on the street, and from the other side of the passage, she saw a light shining, illuminating the main wall of the washhouse. Whiffs of mold and stains drifted from the gloomy vault, a stench of cellars, latrines, rear barracks. We always stopped for a moment there, letting a draft come to us, along with images from our childhood.

Once her memory had reproduced the childish screams she had made in our company during every trip through Liars' Bridge, Maryama Adougaï ventured into the nauseating space. She advanced using the lights in the washhouse's square as a reference point. The wagon's squeaks reverberated beneath the vault. She held her breath to keep from swallowing the stench. The remaining distance had diminished: twenty-five steps at most, a large portion of which were taken in apnea.

She came out into the square and, without glancing at the backdrop, without lifting her eyes toward the dreary buildings, the barbed wire barricades, and condemned streets of Bloc 709, she approached the washhouse.

Beneath the first spigot was an assortment of bottles.

She brought her wagon to the center spigot.

The civil defense soldiers were dozing on an old sofa they had salvaged from an abandoned house on Leel Fourmanova Street. Beneath their feet lay a notebook in which they were supposed to record any incidents along with their watch hours. The sound of the wagon woke them. Wordlessly, they nodded their heads in Maryama Adougaï's direction to let her know that she could take as much water as she pleased.

Maryama Adougaï propped the first jerrican on the grate spanning the furrow, then she loosened the spigot's wheel. The water ran with force, the container was quickly filled to the brim. She shut off the spigot, screwed on the jerrican's cap, heaved it back on the wagon with a pelvic thrust, and was about to pick up the bucket when, suddenly, she saw me.

She had just placed her hand on the bucket's handle. And at that moment, suddenly, she saw me.

Around midnight, I had been thrown onto the spiked barricade. My hands were caught higher in the barbed wire, and I looked like I was trying to mimic a bird with its wings spread, an abnormally large fowl, sprawled and silent within an atrocious net. I was no longer in pain. I had stopped breathing a little after midnight, and I had then decided to stay and watch the coming of dawn. Maryama Adougaï's appearance there made me happy in a way I could have never dared to hope for. As soon as I saw her emerge from the black space of the tunnel, I'd wanted to reveal myself, shake the barbed rampart in order to attract her attention, but I didn't have enough strength.

Maryama Adougaï saw me, exhaled a groan of bleak surprise, and dropped her bucket. She stood up, walked past the soldiers' pitiful sofa, and headed toward me. The soldiers immediately came out of their reverie. The oldest one was already standing.

"Where does she think she's going?" he grumbled.

"That's my brother," Maryama Adougaï explained without stopping. The other man hesitated, then followed in her footsteps.

"No touching, no taking the body," he warned. "He has to stay like that until tomorrow night."

She was now standing before me, three meters away, no closer, though not because she intended to obey the soldier, but because the barbed wire had been trimmed and reinforced over the decades, and now resembled a monstrous and shapeless briar patch, laden with buds and suckers that could sting, rend, and tear at a distance. Lit only by the bulb shining over the washhouse, the scene unfolded in half-darkness. Maryama Adougaï could hardly make out the wire's vicious claws. The only thing she saw clearly was my body, which was right under the light of the lamp, appearing to float between sky and earth, along with, just behind the spiny shrub, an abandoned road, bricked-up windows, rotting roofs, the void.

Since Maryama Adougaï wasn't trying to remove me from where I was, and since she remained quiet and unmoving before me, the soldier made no gestures in her direction, though he did stand nearby to keep an eye on her. Our dialogue was going to unfurl in the presence of an unfriendly ear. The circumstances were dire, but fundamentally the same ones that had determined our behavior since birth. We knew how to cope: talk about something else, speak without speaking, only show emotion in a way incomprehensible to the enemy, leave essential things in the shadows.

"Jean Adougaï," Maryama Adougaï murmured, "I thought they'd taken you to a reeducation center. What are you doing here?"

"I had some problems with the staff," I said. "I fought with them. I didn't want to learn their language."

"Were there casualties, Jean Adougaï?"

"Oh, yes, a few. I couldn't understand what they were asking. They harassed me. I defended myself."

There was a silence.

"What time is it?" I said.

"It's nighttime," Maryama Adougaï replied.

"I'm waiting for dawn," I said.

"You seem well, little brother," Maryama Adougaï remarked.

By Maryama Adougaï's side, the soldier shrugged.

"Have you gone to see Aunt Boyol?" I asked, after a new silence.

"She's feeling fine," Maryama Adougaï said. "She's singing songs, making some final adjustments to our maximum program."

"It's a beautiful program," I said.

"Yes, it's a beautiful program," Maryama Adougaï repeated.

The soldier was growing impatient. He touched my little sister's arm.

"This interview is over," he said gruffly. "She's going back to fill her containers."

"Keep waiting, little brother," Maryama Adougaï murmured.

I would have liked to make a gesture with the tips of my fingers, a gesture of approval and trust, or say something affectionate. But I couldn't manage to do it. Everything was scrambled up in my head. I didn't have much control left.

"It's going to be alright," I said. "I have everything under control." My voice didn't carry. I don't think Maryama Adougaï heard me. "She's going to stop crying now," the soldier insisted. "The interview is over, life goes on. She's going to stop crying. There's nothing she can do now. There's nothing anyone can do. That's how it is."

"Yes, that's how it is," I said.

To bring the scene to a close.

Granny Holgolde's Tale: The Camp

Marta Ashkarot stopped for a moment at the entrance to the camp, just in front of the large gate, then she continued walking and pushed through the barrier with her titanic knees. The ruined gateway was a combination of metal and wood. The iron plates split under the pressure, the planks were already rotted, and an opening was created, but, in order to condemn the path, the last soldiers to pass through had taken care to knit a thick band of barbed wire around the fence, and the elephant was wary of the parts that could still spring up or irrationally attack and cause terrible injury. She especially didn't want to lacerate her trunk and so she took several precautions. The fence and scrap iron resisted for a good half dozen seconds, then crumbled into dust, as if they had been waiting for this intervention to renounce all form and vanish. The splintered wood smelled of mushrooms. The barbed wire also had a strong odor, though rather one of guano and rust. The friable scales scattered without even a single nick. None of the spines on the wire had survived corrosion. The formidable points had become nothing more than inoffensive snowflakes.

Time's taken its toll on this place, Marta Ashkarot thought, as a wave of fatalistic nostalgia washed over her body. Thirty-five, sixty-two, a hundred forty years? For her, untouched by time or death, simply changing homes at the end of her life, such numbers had lost most of their meaning. Her counting of years obeyed increasingly imprecise methods of calculation. What could she have said about the age of this camp? That it had been abandoned for a very, very long time, was all she could say. She knew she was incapable of any sort of dating process attached to reality, so it was better to stick to vague formulations. The camp belonged to a distant epoch, that's all. It had been abandoned, the door had been forever shut and padlocked by its last occupants. Then humidity, lunar acidity, terrestrial gravity, silence, and wind had seen to its disintegration.

In the past, the camp had covered a spectacularly vast surface, and there had once been a period when you could have walked for an entire day in a straight line without reaching either end, but, these days, it was impossible to ascertain its dimensions, as the forest had overtaken the terrain, gradually replacing it over time. Once through the gate, there was no sense of the camp's immensity, only the feeling of being among the ruins of a small backwoods resort, with a few open-air barracks, some permanent houses, and a dispensary. Farther afield, no matter which direction you went, the facilities had been submerged in bamboo, trees, or tall grass. Between the gate and the green, dense, and visibly impenetrable barricade standing two hundred meters away, a street had survived, despite everything. It must be the main road, leading to official accommodations and administrative buildings, as well as the pavilion where distinguished guests were lodged when they arrived from the capital.

Marta Ashkarot advanced slowly along this path. On both her right and left, the view was the same: collapsed constructions that were hardly recognizable from their glory days, and houses with shattered windows, filled with dirt, from which sprouted abundant, evil-looking tufts, creepers, and shrubs. The camp may have experienced a period of at least partial repopulation, as here and there on crumbled roofs you could see remnants of tarps, the traces of an attempt at reclaiming the ruins, but, at present, everything was deserted. There was a heavy silence. Even the monkeys had decided to avoid this place, and their cries were extremely distant, nearly inaudible.

Marta Ashkarot had just traveled five hundred meters and was about to turn onto a second street, also overgrown and lined with demolished houses, when a face materialized without warning in her field of vision.

It was a human face. Thirty meters away, an old man had passed by a window and turned toward the newcomer, in an attitude that expressed a stupefaction so strong it almost looked sorrowful. The old man was blind. His body floated within a tattered uniform, and, in suitable places, his head and hands emerged, discolored by the same disastrous shade of tropical humus.

The small house that the man occupied seemed to have sunk askew into the earth. He had evacuated a considerable amount of rubble in order to make the space habitable, chaotically disseminating it all around the base of the outer walls of his abode, like a series of disheveled molehills. Following the definitive collapse of the roof, shelter had been secured by a structure of khaki canvas, patched haphazardly according to an approximative, poor-sighted technique.

"Is that you, Volodia?" the man suddenly asked, breaking from the petrification that had characterized him until that point.

Marta Ashkarot didn't respond. She felt she had nothing to respond with. She stood still. She breathed in information through the tip of her trunk, trying to understand just who this unknown blind man was and what he wanted.

The man looked like a young soldier from the Chinese Cultural Revolution who had let nearly three-quarters of a century pass without ever dreaming of changing his outfit. He washed his clothes regularly enough, and surely had the camp's military laundry at his disposition to restore his padded jacket for the past five or ten years, but his tastes in fashion had remained the same. He had grown old in this uniform, he had become decrepit inside it, and it was where he had encountered his first attacks of blindness, followed later by the permanent darkening of his retinas.

Marta Ashkarot took a few steps forward. The stranger had surmised a presence, but was incapable of grasping its form. His features expressed anxiety and uncertainty. The elephant blew a double note through her long nostrils to test his auditive capacities, as well as to identify herself as an intelligent animal, heavy but inoffensive. This sound wasn't a trumpet, but its origin could hardly be mistaken. The stranger didn't react. There was no additional strain on his face. He had heard nothing. It seemed that the blind old man was hard of hearing as well.

Moved by a feeling of compassion, Marta Ashkarot was about to speak when the man continued talking, repeating his question from a minute ago.

"Is that you, Volodia?" he repeated. "I've been waiting for you. I knew we'd see each other again someday."

Marta Ashkarot walked up to the house, skirted past one of the molehills, and planted herself in front of the window, a few steps away from the ledge on which the man was leaning.

She was now curiously observing his octogenarian face, eroded by fate and a solitary life amid nature. She evaluated his survivor's body. He was tanned, mummified, but appeared solid. His teeth, for example, had resisted the ravages of time. If no great climatic catastrophe occurred, and if the wars of extermination didn't reach this region in the coming years, this individual could still hold on for at least another decade.

"I knew you'd come back, Volodia," the old man continued. "I knew you'd come back to demand an explanation from me. I waited for you. I'll tell you everything."

Marta Ashkarot flapped her ears to chase away the flies and mosquitoes buzzing around her head. It had rained during the night and, taking advantage of the sun's return, insects were everywhere.

They witnessed the scene, though without any particular appreciation of it, purely as parasites.

"Do you see the state you left me in?" the old man said. "A whole life has gone by. It was as cruel for you as it was for me. Do you see what I've become? Do you see, Volodia?"

"Of course," Marta Ashkarot said.

The old man's expression turned sullen.

"It wasn't easy for you or for me," he said.

The elephant glanced around. She found this conversation unpleasant and was already thinking about taking off. At the first intersection, the camp merged with the forest. Banana and mango trees stood at the vanguard, and beyond there was nothing but an indescribable clutter.

"I know you're annoyed with me," the old man said. "You've always thought it was me who denounced you as a rightist. You thought I was a conspirator in the whole ordeal."

"Ah," Marta Ashkarot said.

"Don't you remember?" the old man shouted. "You accused me of denouncing you, you showered me with insults in front of everyone. And then they took you away and you disappeared."

Leaning on the window, the old man became agitated. He seemed to be sniffing the air to determine the location of his interlocutor. He cast his glassy eyes about at random, on targets distant or close, on clouds, on anthills, on the elephant, to no avail. He had lifted up an arm as if to point out something. He pointed at nothing. His face expressed anxiety, confusion, and anger all at once.

"Well it wasn't me. Do you remember Irina? Fat Irina?"

"No," the elephant said.

"My wife, at the time. Dammit, Volodia, try to remember! She was the committee secretary. Remember now?"

"Oh, yes," Marta Ashkarot said. "Fat Irina."

"She's the one who denounced you," the old man sighed, sweeping away mosquitos with his right hand. "She's the one who wrote the first report against you. It wasn't me. But then things got out of hand."

Marta Ashkarot let out a rumble. It was to punctuate the stranger's soliloquy and encourage him to give more details.

"Then, you know how it goes," the old man said. "We all started making reports against each other. Things got out of hand. But the first one was written by her. Fat Irina. It was her. The first denunciation."

"And now," Marta Ashkarot remarked, "you're denouncing your wife."

She was no longer making an effort to disguise her voice and, even if the stranger was hard of hearing, he was suddenly taken with doubt.

"Is that you, Volodia?" he asked, rubbing his face, as if he had just smelled a whiff of sulfuric or acidic gas.

Marta Ashkarot shrugged. She was preparing to leave back through where she had come from and didn't want to participate anymore in this exchange.

"Is that you, Volodia?" the stranger asked again. "Why won't you answer me?"

She gazed at the gray, heavy sky, the empty clouds. There were no birds above the forest. She had begun to turn around.

"It wasn't easy for anyone," the old man said in an aggressive tone. "Don't think you were the only one to suffer, Volodia. Everyone's had a hard time of it."

He paused. The elephant had stopped in her U-turn. She felt as though he were going to add something important. She was no longer looking at him, but she continued to listen.

"Huh? What did you say?" the old man asked.

"Nothing," the elephant let slip.

"Everyone's had a really hard time of it," the stranger grumbled. "But at least it wasn't for nothing."

In the common room, whenever the schoolteacher was arrested or killed, there was a Red soldier who often gave us our lessons. There were always new teachers, but, in the interims, he was called in. The man's name was Schumann; he had lost his right arm in combat on the frontlines of Orbise, he had to be in his thirties, and his scientific knowledge was just barely greater than our own. Pedagogically speaking, I don't think I'm exaggerating when I say that he was useless. Since we were young, we didn't really notice, but, thinking back on it, yes, he was useless.

He paced in front of the blackboard, brandishing a piece of chalk in his left hand and avoiding like the plague the fatal moment when he would have to write something. Although he was not literate enough to have orthographical standards, he instinctively felt that it would be better not to impose on us his laborious drawings, and, when he finally had to do so, he pondered for several long seconds between each stroke, all while exasperatedly wiping his forehead which was suddenly glistening with sweat.

His lessons were initially about instilling us with military discipline. Then came classes on arithmetic. We tediously repeated operations that we had memorized months before. We were called to endlessly recite multiplication tables in an even rhythm that Soldier Schumann marked by nodding in assent, with a severe and silent satisfaction. As soon as the count reached fifty, we would notice our teacher getting slightly embarrassed and, after sixty, he abandoned the exercise, to our delight. Elli Zlank was the only one among us who knew how to multiply eights and nines. He picked up the slack in our voices when we started to flag, and, even when he made a mistake, Soldier Schumann continued to eruditely move his head, paying foremost attention to the melody, but also to the natural authority of the best student and, anyhow, unable to correct any sort of mathematical error.

After this immersion in numbers, Schumann drifted toward subjects in which he was much better versed: hand-to-hand combat skills and basic egalitarian ideology. We learned from him how to wield a bayonet, slit a guard's throat at night, and use only your left arm to strike an enemy's vital organs. Then, black with dust, exhausted from falling down, and bruised from mutually-inflicted blows, we returned to our desks and listened to what he had to say on political theory.

Soldier Schumann taught us what he knew, which is to say an amalgamation of popular Marxism useful for making decisions and choosing a side during strikes and armed conflicts. However, since he lodged in a barracks for invalids, among whom included several Tibetans, he had been subjected to a powerful Buddhist influence as well, altering his language. After his lecture, we had to recite the Ten Precious April Theses, the Five Noble Differences Between Socialism and Communism, the Twelve Luminous Proletarian Virtues, not to mention our favorite list: the Nine Stinking Categories.

Schumann only really excelled in one domain: singing. He had no grounding in music theory, but his baritone voice was tuned and moving, and he was keen to make us sing along with him. In the poorly lit, poorly ventilated classroom, which despite the board and desks resembled more a storeroom than a place of study, our choir created for just a few moments a haven of beauty. We started with revolutionary classics and war hymns meant to galvanize across barricades and trenches, but Schumann quickly broached a lyrical repertoire belonging to another world, a defunct world, the world of the First Soviet Union, which for some reason he clearly preferred to the Second. The Russian, Ukrainian, or Georgian harmonies swept away the ugliness of our daily lives, their languor transported us to the heart of a land where emotion reigned supreme. Our songs evoked abandoned peasants, snowy moonlit trails, the wounded and dying, entrusting to a crow one last amorous thought, one final yearning. Even on the cheeks of little Marsyas Grodnoll, who claimed to hate music and sang out of tune, there would be tears. Marsyas Grodnoll would go sit apart from everyone else so as not to ruin our perfect chords. He would shut his mouth, lower his head, and cry.

Outside these miraculous sessions, class under Soldier Schumann's direction was a series of tiresome moments. It could also be dangerous.

Schumann's teaching was disorganized, and we often had trouble adjusting to his changes in subject, his digressions, and his sudden outbursts. He demanded an iron discipline from us: for example, he forbade us from speaking up to ask for clarification when we missed something he said. It was better, incidentally, only to interrupt when he knew the answer to the question we were going to ask. School days were composed mainly of evasive, confused monologues and periods of choir practice. We had to remain rigid and unmoving until recess time. This, in the absence of a schoolyard, was in the same room where we had just been listening to the master. We dedicated this half hour of rest to practicing bayonet attacks and close-combat techniques for the physically impaired, which, obviously, temporarily turned the room into a chaotic fighting ring. We would finish recess exhausted, to once again listen to Schumann rant with neither order nor end about the causes of the defeats he had experienced, the unionizing of factory workers and peasants, the critical growth of productive forces, and the physiology of amputees, including that unbearable itchiness one-armed people continue to feel in their missing limb.

I mentioned that class could be dangerous. It was for me on the same day the bombings started again.

Schumann was in the middle of explaining, for the umpteenth time, the causes and consequences of the itching sensations that plagued his nonexistent hand, when I noticed a tiny black shape inching down toward the opening of his empty sleeve. It was a millipede like the ones you could find crawling around the yard or even in the barracks. This one was small. I was sitting in the front row and I know that other students must have spotted the arthropod as well. We watched this spectacle, fascinated but disciplined enough not to show our excitement, as it added an unexpected spice to the monotonous drone. Schumann was leaning against the wall two meters away from us while he spoke. I think he had been drinking, since we could occasionally smell his warm breath, which carried a lingering whiff of beer. Schumann's jacket was a dirty greatcoat made of felt, in a faded gray khaki. Our teacher gave off the impression that he had just returned from the frontlines and was still steeped in the heroic horrors, mud, and blood of combat. This infantry jacket weighed down his movements, and when he chose to stand still instead of pacing in front of us, his hanging sleeve didn't move more than a millimeter. I exchanged a glance with Rita Mirvrakis. We admired the arthropod's insolence and tranquility. Before plunging into the sleeve, it explored the opening. Then it entered and disappeared.

"It's from a wound," Schumann explained. "Oh, yes . . . a surprise wound . . . The doctors say the nerves are talking . . . But what nerves, since they've all been cut off? . . . Huh? . . . What nerves, I ask you? . . . Well, I ask you, but you don't know . . . you don't know anything . . . I'm the only one with this pain . . . no one else . . . My commander, Baalbal, was amputated too . . . Commander Jean Baalbal . . . an officer who refused to wear any sort of stripe on his uniform . . . dressed like us . . . in the same boat . . . battle-hardened . . . Now there's a man who knew the Ten Precious April Theses like the back of his hand . . . Not like you ignorant bunch . . . Jean Baalbal . . . a diehard egalitarian . . . A shame you never knew him . . . you could've used a role model like him . . . He lost a foot . . . torn to shreds . . . I was next to him, I hadn't lost my arm yet . . . That I lost an hour later . . . He continued commanding, even with a mangled foot . . . despite the pain . . . he only had a few

pieces of meat hanging from his pant leg . . . it didn't look like anything . . . you had to see it . . . it looked like these . . . strips . . . He
was lying on a heap of gravel . . . He kept giving orders, refused to
be evacuated . . . Evacuated where, I ask you? . . . Well, I ask, but I
know you can't answer . . . We didn't have a backup base . . . the
military hospital was in flames . . . there was a general hospital for
civilians twenty kilometers away, in some conurbation whose name
I forget . . . Civilian hospitals are more lacking in equipment than
army latrines . . . It goes to show . . . My commander, Jean Baalbal,
was lying on his heap of pebbles . . . It was pretty funny, seeing our
commander with only one shoe . . . Spread out on the blood-soaked
gravel . . . He kept directing the battle . . . Yes sir, commander! . . . Jean Baalbal . . . At your command! . . . Then it was my
turn . . . An explosion, then I couldn't see a thing . . . For a moment
I didn't even know if I was still alive . . . Both of us were finally taken
to the hospital . . . I can't recall the town's name . . . Anyway, you
don't care . . . little ingrates . . . You're the ones we were fighting
for . . . not just for you, but for you too . . . Dunces . . . You don't
care, you don't know anything . . . They brought us both
there . . . They cut off his leg above the knee . . . Like with me they
got him drunk before the operation . . . They got us plastered since
they didn't have any drugs . . . The place had nothing . . . No instru-
ments, no anesthesia, nothing . . . Do you know what anesthesia
is? . . . No, obviously you don't . . . you know nothing about nothing,
have to teach you everything . . . Have to talk to you like you're
babies . . . Anesthesia is how you don't feel anything when the surgeon is sawing off one of your limbs . . . You hear everything, but
you don't feel a thing . . . That's anesthesia . . . When the saw gets to
the bone, you feel the vibrations in your body, but there's no
pain . . . Since there wasn't any anesthesia they made us drink until
we passed out . . . We were next to each other on mattresses, Commander Jean Baalbal and I . . . we woke up with hangovers . . . You

don't know what a hangover is either . . . you're all just little green-horns, no knowledge at all . . . We woke up like we'd just gotten blitzed . . . We were in a hospital corridor . . . We smelled like vomit, burnt stuff, rotting flesh, blood . . . Luckily, there was also the smell of gauze . . . I don't know why, but I've always liked the smell of gauze . . . it smells clean, like a pharmacy . . . I didn't even know they'd cut off my arm yet . . . It was a shock to find that out . . . yes, it's one hell of a shock . . . You couldn't understand . . . No one could understand unless they've had to get an amputation . . . Maybe you'll get it one day . . . if it happens to you . . . When it's your head that's cut off, at least you don't have anything to complain about anymore . . . There's no unpleasant awakening . . . The head, at least, has that advantage . . . But when it's your arm, or leg . . . or your virile member . . . You all know what a virile member is . . . you obviously know about that, you pigs . . . At your age, I knew about everything . . . Virile members were my favorite subject . . . no reason you'd be any different now . . . Well? . . . Nothing to say now? . . . Sure you all think about that more than the Twelve Luminous Proletarian Virtues . . . Boys and girls both . . . You're all the same . . . Anyway, they didn't cut off my virile member, they cut off my right arm . . . not my commander's virile member either . . . just his leg . . . cut it above the knee, after a few hours lying on gravel it got infected . . . Infection, gangrene, that's what does you in . . . you think you've lost a foot but then you've got to get cut up all the way to your thigh . . . Infection is why the surgeon has to cut more off . . . The commander had a pretty bad infection, and I was at risk too . . . they grabbed everything they had for knives and saws and had no problem cutting more off . . . Jean Baalbal . . . an officer of steel . . . a model of heroism . . . Yes sir, commander! . . . Soldier Schumann, reporting for duty! . . . They sawed off his leg all the way up to his ass . . . They cut me off at the armpit . . . We woke up at the same time . . . The first few minutes are the worst . . . You're overwhelmed, you want to vomit, you want to die . . . Like it's so important to have all your limbs . . . Luckily, you hang on . . . You want to die, but you hang on . . . After the first shock there's always someone who wants to talk to you . . . so you hang on to what he says . . . You'll see, if it happens to you . . . Schumann, the commander said, stop hollering, like it's so important to have all your limbs . . . the important thing is having enough to fight . . . the important thing is the Five Noble Differences Between Socialism and Communism . . . the important thing is the April Theses . . . I was all sprawled out my mattress, surrounded by the smell of rotting meat, blood . . . Luckily, I only had to turn on my side to sniff the gauze on my shoulder . . . it kept me calm . . . You know what sprawled means? . . . It means sick, disgusted, unable to move . . . not wanting anything . . . You'll see, it'll happen to you one day or another . . . you'll be sprawled on an old mattress . . . We spent the day like that, hollering, one of us or the other . . . then we simmered down . . . My hand itched . . . my right hand, the missing one . . . it tingled, burned, ached . . . Commander, I asked, do you feel anything in your leg? . . . any ants, does it itch? . . . What leg, what are you asking, Schumann? . . . Commander, I said, my missing arm hurts . . . it's like there's two hundred mosquitos on it all sucking out my blood . . . On your missing arm? He asked . . . I told him yes . . . maybe not two hundred, but a lot . . . say a hundred fifty . . . they're biting me and I can't swat them . . . there's nothing for me to scratch . . . my arm doesn't exist anymore, it's in the trash, with the wads of dirty cotton . . . or in the Meat Bardo . . . My commander started shouting at me . . . Soldier Schumann! He shouted . . . Soldier Schumann, stop bellowing nonsense, your arm is done with, mosquitoes aren't biting it anymore, what are you talking about? . . . The important thing isn't to swat mosquitoes, it's to swat the enemy . . . swat the enemy into oblivion . . . get on the fast track to building a classless society . . . What is there to do for the tingling in your phantom arm? . . . Do you think I'm wasting my time thinking about my phantom leg right now? . . . I'm reciting the Seven

Perfect Principles of Revolutionary Dictatorship to myself, better than thinking about mosquitoes! . . . That's what Commander Jean Baalbal said to me . . . The Seven Perfect Principles of Revolutionary Dictatorship . . . I'll have to teach you that one of these days . . . So anyway, I never found out if his foot was itching or not . . . We recited the Seven Perfect Principles of Revolutionary Dictatorship together, then the Eight Spectacular Steps To Reach a Classless Society . . . we recited them all night long . . . Then, he came down with a fever . . . and forty-eight hours later, he died . . . Jean Baalbal, was his name . . . Remember that name . . . Commander Jean Baalbal . . . The best of all of us . . . Maybe he reacted just like me to his missing limb's itch . . . The nurses say the itching really does exist . . . a heavy feeling in my shoulder, too, a pang, like everything's still in place . . . They say it's a natural phenomenon, that it's the nerves talking . . . But what nerves, huh? . . . The only nerve people know about, the only one everyone talks about is the optical nerve . . . That's not a mystery to anyone . . . Even you've heard of it . . . It's all anyone talks about . . . Even you dunces . . . The optical nerve is tied to the eye . . . it's the rest of the eye, in the back, goes right to the brain . . . But don't tell me there's an armical nerve or a legical nerve . . . right from the shoulder to the brain, right from the thigh to the brain . . . that's unthinkable . . . There's no nerve like that . . . Well . . . No, there's no nerve like that . . . If a nonexistent hand starts itching, maybe the nerves are talking, but it's mainly a mystery of nature . . . Once we have Communism, there'll be no more mysteries . . . nature will be entirely conquered by humans and subhumans . . . we'll know how to stop the tingling in phantom hands . . . we'll master the armical and legical nerves . . . And we won't amputate the wounded by filling them up with alcohol instead of anesthetics . . ."

At that moment, I made the idiotic mistake of raising my hand. Soldier Schumann noticed my finger in the air. After his long deluge of a monologue, he doubtlessly felt the need to take a break. He stopped talking and knitted his brows irately, daring me to ask my question.

"Teacher," I asked. "Do you feel ants right now?"

He hesitated. Schumann had always suspected that I was a troublemaker. As soon as I spoke, the studious atmosphere grew tense, the students clearly preparing for something. No one knew where my question was heading. The whole room was waiting with bated breath. Schumann still didn't have enough information to decide whether my words were out of mere curiosity, a desire for extra clarification, or deviousness. He glared at me.

"Yes," he finally said.

"Those aren't ants," I said. "It's no mystery at all. There's a millipede up your sleeve."

Laughter broke out. The back rows, who hadn't seen the bug crawl into Schumann's clothes, interpreted my outburst as rambunctious insolence. Next to me, shaking her desk, Rita Mirvrakis was guffawing.

Schumann peeled himself off the wall. He had turned red. He approached the first row like he was going to kill me. Rita Mirvrakis went quiet.

Everyone went quiet.

I was eight years old. I didn't want to get hurt and I could feel tears welling up in my eyes. An adult was advancing toward me in order to beat me to death with the unstoppable techniques of an invalid. I began stammering urgently.

"It's true," I said, "A millipede . . . A millipede went into your arm . . . Well . . . in . . . into your sleeve . . . I'm not lying . . ."

Soldier Schumann towered over me with all his height. I had hidden my head between my shoulders so as to die faster when Schumann would ultimately strike a pressure point, with a suddenly-produced bayonet or his left fist. I smelled the stench of his dirty felt jacket, the lingering odors of the barracks, foul mess halls. Schumann's body gave off a rotten smell as well.

"Özbeg," Schumann shouted, not killing me, "since the beginning, you have been a member of the Ninth Stinking Category! You and Mirvrakis, I don't want to see either of you ever again! Get out! Get your packs and scram!"

"I didn't do anything," Rita Mirvrakis protested, sniffling.

Schumann ignored her. I'm sure he wanted to kill her too. But in the camp, among the remaining proletarian virtues, there was one that let hope rest on children. We were threatened, we were disparaged, we were shown little affection, we weren't spared criticism, we were punished, but no one ever touched a hair on our heads. There were no beaten children in the Negrini Bloc or any other. Schumann, of course, obeyed this collective rule. Our own did not beat or kill us. Only the enemy had that privilege.

"I don't want to see either of you ever again!" he brayed. "Ever! Out! Scram! Out! . . ."

Once the door had closed behind us, the first thing Rita Mirvrakis did was slap me.

"It's your fault we both got punished," she raged.

I rubbed my burning cheek in silence. When Rita Mirvrakis slapped you, she didn't hold back.

"I thought he was going to kill me," I said in a breath.

Rita Mirvrakis shrugged her small shoulders. She was two years older than me, she towered over me by a head, but she had small shoulders.

"He should've," she shot back.

"What?" I asked, dreading the ensuing confirmation, but unable to admit that Rita Mirvrakis might wish me that much harm. "Should've what?"

My voice was bloodless, but I was holding back my tears.

"Killed you," she confirmed coldly.

60

I harbored a more than fraternal affection for Rita Mirvrakis, and she knew it. She saw that her retort had hurt me. Distraught, frozen, I was about to sob. She touched my arm and changed her tone.

"I'm joking," she said. "Idiot."

Rita Mirvrakis had witnessed the decapitation and burning of her family, specifically her grandmother, one of her mothers, an aunt, her brothers. Adopted by neighbors in Camp 801, she lived more or less normally for about two years, until her replacement parents were arrested during a genetic conformity inspection. She then ended up with us, in the children's section of the Molinari Barracks, although she might have preferred the women's dormitory. These numerous experiences had hardened her, or rather, had given her an anxious personality, which for the most part she successfully hid behind a haughty, meanish coldness, though she couldn't always control it. That's when she would suffer fits. Without warning, she would lose consciousness of her surroundings and wall herself off, unspeaking, or conversely, babbling continuously for an hour or two, an outpouring of her delirium. She would inundate us with her dark visions and nightmares. This frightened the other children, who quickly shrank away from her, but I stayed nearby until she came back to reality. I have to say that we had a special connection. With me, she could set aside her coldness and even be tender. She knew that she flustered me, but, instead of making fun of me or stringing me along, she accepted me by her side as if I were her little brother. She needed someone to lean on, like all of us. Nighttime in the Molinari Barracks allowed us to deepen our complicity. We'd often meet in her bed and, before falling asleep next to each other, we'd talk about the world into which we'd been born, retelling Granny Holgolde's tales, inventing stories of vengeance and imagining better worlds where we were the heroes—and where nonetheless, despite our efforts, everything ended terribly.

"You saw the millipede too, right?" I asked.

"Yes," she said. "But you can't tell the teacher that."

Our quarrel ended there. Once again we were like brother and sister, a pair of juvenile outcasts, two punished delinquents who didn't really know what their punishment was supposed to be. Expulsion from class was an extraordinary situation. Soldier Schumann had innovated with us, and, on the scale of consequences, this was unprecedented, outlandish even. We had never imagined it before and had no idea what to do with it.

"Where do we go now?" I asked.

"I don't know," Rita Mirvrakis said.

Around us, the street was dark. The classroom was located in a sub-basement of the meeting hall, and, after a flight of steps, we exited directly into the city. We had a choice: return to the hall, wander the empty barracks and rest homes for invalids and the mentally ill, risk being reprimanded by the nurse's aides and the insane, or go on an adventure—first to the heart of the Harkovat District, then beyond, to the Kanal and even further, to places that were not totally unknown to us but which we had never visited outside parades, under guardian supervision.

Rita Mirvrakis grabbed the fingers of my right hand for a few seconds and dragged me along. She'd decided to venture into unexplored territories. Then she let go of my hand and I began to walk beside her.

"What if the director sees us?" I asked worriedly.

"We'll tell her we're going to buy some milk."

"Milk?"

"Yes, we'll tell her that the soldier sent us out for a can of milk. For a lesson."

"Oh," I said skeptically.

"A lesson on poisons and antidotes. She'll believe us."

"What if she doesn't?" I objected.

"We'll kill her."

I turned toward her and stared into her eyes. They were cloudy, like whenever she discharged odd images, terrible images, frightening images, like during her delirious episodes.

"We'll drown her in milk, in poison," she muttered through her teeth, more to herself than to me. "In a puddle of poison. We'll lay her down next to the soldier and decapitate them both."

"We don't have a knife," I objected.

"We'll decapitate them by hand, with our teeth," she muttered.

There was nothing particularly abnormal about Rita Mirvrakis's intonations. I withdrew into myself for a few minutes. I felt like I couldn't tell if I was awake or if I had plunged into a new dream, into a place more nightmarish, more oneiric, than my real existence. I no longer knew at what level of reality to place myself. I don't know about you, but it's something I wondered about regularly at the time and, same as today, I never could be at all certain.

The streets came one after another. Alley 488. Alley 489. Noura Slaheer Street. Thilmiya Grootz Street. Ogoussone Thoroughfare. Alley 604. Loudjima Mahaorian Street. Jean and Mariya Harfalar Street.

Street followed street. They were littered with garbage, vibrant with fetidity, with sordid recollections.

"What if we went to Granny Holgolde's?" I suggested.

"Do you know where she lives?" Rita Mirvrakis shot back.

"No," I confessed.

My companion stared at me with dismay.

"What if we went to Granny Holgolde's?" she aped.

"Fine," I said, annoyed.

"Idiot," she said.

We'd left the Harkovat District behind us, passing by indistinct buildings, abandoned worksites, where it was impossible to tell if they were in the middle of demolition or reconstruction. We walked for hours. Sometimes, for two or three hundred meters, the streets would be bustling. Vagrants, semi-vagrants, closed-face proletarians, guardsmen, guardswomen, all kinds of crippled people, men, women, uniformed supervisors, all heading to their mysterious destinations, saying nothing to us. They were indifferent to our presence. Or maybe, if this turned out to be a dream, we didn't have enough substance to attract their attention. In any case, the disregard in which we were held felt quite comfortable to us. We had no problem walking on twilit sidewalks when there were sidewalks, avoiding collision with objects and the living.

"By the way, are you still there, Rita?" Rita Mirvrakis asked herself quietly. "Don't you think it stinks here? Huh? . . . You don't smell that? . . ."

She was talking to herself, as she often did, making up questions and their answers, sometimes developing one point or another, or an image, in considerable detail, unconcerned with my opinion or even proof that someone was listening to her.

The city did stink. We didn't mind leaving the hall's poorly lit corridors and tunnels behind, or going outside into the open air, but the open air in question carried with it all the bad odors that pervaded our dead-end world; it mixed together the effluvia of prisons and camps, the stench of black war, covert or brutal depending on the season, the musk of the war's bombs, barbed-wire fences, chemical dustings, still-smoking ruins nearby, ruins that stopped smoking decades ago, content with giving off memories of fire and wailing: all these smells combined as well with the odors of nurseries and hospices for subhumans, the wind of distress, repressed or vivid and unhealed, the flatulence of this world, flatulence that spoke of the suffering of nearly everyone around us and elsewhere. That was what we inhaled into our always-open mouths in the camp or during our trips to town. And, doubtlessly because we had just thought of it, we felt as if at this very moment it carried fresh smells, like a

64

completely new horror that had suddenly and violently insinuated itself into our nostrils.

"Well, Rita, I think it absolutely stinks," Rita Mirvrakis continued in the same tone. "Of course it stinks . . . it smells bad and it'll always smell bad . . . How could it be any different . . . Tardaz Street, Kam Yip Street, piles of dirty clothes . . . Albert Trott Street, the city morgue . . . Varkaunas Street, butcher's shops . . . collapsed houses . . . Holger Schmidt Street, the refugee barracks. . ."

She listed a few more places, then she was quiet.

"We might still not be far from Granny Holgolde's," I said. "I recognize one of the places I went to once, with Aunt Kirkuk and Soldier Robmann."

Rita Mirvrakis stopped to scrutinize the area. She looked both lost and like she didn't care.

"I don't remember Soldier Robmann," she said. "I don't remember coming here with Aunt Kirkuk."

We were next to an intersection. I went to read what the signs said. They were high up and faded. Ounda Street, Vincents-Sanchaise Street. I returned to Rita and gave my report.

"Vincents-Sanchaise Street," she repeated. "Fine. We'll go there."

"To Granny Holgolde's house?" I asked.

"No, idiot," Rita Mirvrakis said. "Granny Holgolde moved into a sovkhoz. It's not anywhere near here. Just the opposite. It's basically in the countryside. Don't you remember when we went there? We had to get in a van. We rode for a long time. It's outside the city, kilometers away."

"I don't remember," I said.

Stepping onto Vincents-Sanchaise Street, we started talking about what our memory could contain, what it stored askew, accumulated memories that never came out again, false memories. It was a conversation with which we were familiar. Both of us complained about our poor memory. We complained about the tricks it played on us. Oftentimes, no matter what images we had to recall that should have been immediately available to us, nothing came. We had to invent them.

"I don't even remember my birth," Rita Mirvrakis ended up saying. "Same for whatever happened next. Everything's all scrambled up to today. It's a mishmash of images that aren't really real. It's like I don't have a past I can actually believe in."

"Me too," I said.

"What do you mean, you too?" She stopped.

"It's like . . . like I can't . . ." I stammered.

"It's like he can't!" she mocked.

"Uh . . ." I continued. "Like I can't . . . can't really believe in what came before . . ."

"Idiot," she said.

Evening loomed. The already-weak light was dimming. The rag heaps brushing against us lost even more of their faces, and, even more often, smelled of sweat, of rust, of working in mud and dust, of blood.

"It's what'll come next that you shouldn't believe in," Rita Mirvrakis suddenly said.

"Oh," I said, wary.

Wary, or maybe stricken with idiocy, actually.

"You also shouldn't believe in what there is during," Rita Mirvrakis added. "The images we see while our eyes are open. It's better not to believe in the present."

Vincents-Sanchaise Street had a bad reputation. Whenever they mentioned it, the adults claimed that it was easy to get lost there, and that also the enemy had spies there disguised as subhumans who reported to camp authorities, regularly updating the list of surviving Ybürs and Bolshevist sympathizers. It was a dark, winding street, sometimes wide, sometimes reduced to an ill-defined corridor between two grimy walls. It seemed to not have an end, continuing with the same name at intersections in whichever direction you decided to go. The entrances to barracks and houses weren't lit, and, though the shops were always open, they were behind wavy, half-lowered metal shutters that rid them of any attractive qualities. At night, passersby looked like roving animals, prisoners, dressed in tatters and mired in frightening, grouchy meditation. I think it would have been wiser to call it the Vincents-Sanchaise District, since there was once a time when the side streets, alleys, and avenues all shared the same name. We walked throughout for half an hour, with lumps in our throats from the dread of getting lost, our heads full of awful imagery. It involved all manner of harsh punishments and bodily injuries.

"I believe we're lost," I finally said.

"I told you, don't believe anything," Rita Mirvrakis replied.

At that same moment, there was the whistling of a bomb falling from the sky in the distance, then, after a few seconds, an explosion. There was only one detonation—this particular attack wasn't very important. The iron shutters near us trembled, and we could hear annoyed exclamations from the other side of the walls.

Suddenly, the street was empty.

The street. Suddenly. It had emptied of passersby. No more rags approached or followed us.

A troubling street, more than dusky now. The rutted pavement, illuminated by the brush of lights from the half-closed stores. And already the memory of the bomb that faded and transformed, only leaving us with questions without answers. And no one.

"What if the war's started again?" I whispered.

I could barely see Rita Mirvrakis. Rather than keep walking, she had sunk into the entryway of a small apartment. Against the wall dangled a plastic envelope. Inside it was a list. Rita Mirvrakis raised herself up on the tips of her toes and struggled to decipher the names of the residents.

She turned back toward me and sighed.

"The war never ended," she said. "It has no reason to end."

I made an objection. For years, we'd enjoyed a relative calm. Alarms and gunfire were rare.

"It can only keep on going," she added. "And we're in it until we die."

"What are you looking for?" I asked.

"An aunt's name. My parents said that I had an aunt on Vincents-Sanchaise Street, and that she could take care of me in an emergency."

"Which of your parents?" I asked.

"I don't remember," said Rita Mirvrakis. "I was young. Maybe the first ones, maybe the second."

"Is that why we're on Vincents-Sanchaise Street?" I asked.

"Yes, that's why," she said.

"Can she take care of me too?" I asked apprehensively.

"Idiot," Rita Mirvrakis exhaled. "Obviously. We're together."

I huddled next to Rita Mirvrakis and tried to read the names on the list with her.

"What was her name?" I asked.

"Daadza Bourbal." Rita Mirvrakis hesitated. "I'm not really sure. I was little. Daadza or Irma."

We were crossing over into darkness, with all the more difficulty since the sheet—a list of names just like the thousand, ten thousand even, others that existed in the camp—was above our height. Despite the dampness, the ink wasn't smeared too badly. The names were followed by recent dates. I suppose they were more likely disappearance dates than move-in dates.

"There's no Daadza Bourbal in this house," Rita Mirvrakis finally said.

"We'll have to look somewhere else," I proposed.

The notion that an aunt was going to take care of us rested on empty hopes, but I liked it. I felt like I could examine dozens of resident lists in the dark.

"We only had a one in a thousand chance of finding her," Rita Mirvrakis commented. "We didn't find her, that's all. We'll never find her."

"Oh," I said.

"We're still going to look some more, but we won't find her," Rita Mirvrakis said.

"She might be dead, too," I observed.

I wasn't thinking about the possible death of this Daadza Bourbal, I just wanted to agree wholeheartedly with whatever my friend was thinking. I was agreeing at random.

"We're going to look for her some more," Rita Mirvrakis repeated.

Intent on consulting a new list, we directed ourselves toward the entrance of the nearest apartment. On the way, from a space between the two buildings, someone called out to us. There was a small workshop hidden behind a metal curtain. Cut off by the sheet was an open door. It revealed a place of diminished size, cluttered with scrap iron and dismantled objects, doused in yellowy light by a neon tube. In the midst of this bric-a-brac presided a man. He was sitting on a car seat held in place by makeshift wedges, among which we noticed the carcass of a radio transmitter and the remains of a baby stroller. One second was enough to classify this individual as one of the disheartened who had nothing left to lose. He was, in any case, depressed enough to continue, despite his defeat and poor state of dress, wearing his old uniform. He wasn't sporting any medals, but his chest was bedecked with charms and talismans. All around this character were piled cardboard boxes, utensils, engine parts, bits of furniture, and old rags. Right at the moment when he addressed us, a porcelain door-handle had loudly fallen to the pyramid's base, and now, instead of engaging in conversation with us, he was stooped over and picking it up while grumbling to himself. I think he was somewhere between forty and fifty years old, but his shaved head and craggy face, marked by the pains of war, made him appear much older.

We examined him from the street, trying to determine whether he was unhinged or friendly. We considered the appalling stories that blackened Vincents-Sanchaise Street's reputation: child-killers, dark magic, cannibalism. Given the current time and lack of other people around, we should have run far in the opposite direction, but we hesitated. In general, when an adult called out to us, we'd politely freeze and wait to learn more; it's how we'd been brought up.

"Who is that?" I whispered.

"I don't know," Rita Mirvrakis muttered. "It's a soldier."

"What does he want?"

"No clue."

The demobilizee had just stood up. He'd placed the handle by his side. It was very damaged.

"You children look like you're looking for something," he said, his voice deep, weary, a little cracked.

We could now better see his devastated face, the short gray hairs on his bristly skull, his thin cheeks, his tired, strung-out ascetic's gaze. His uniform was too big for his size and was covered in stains. His sad eyes landed on me, then, so as not to frighten me, turned away.

Can I help you? They seemed to say.

Rita Mirvrakis gave me a nudge. She'd decided that we could trust this man.

"We're looking for someone," she said, sidling into the workshop.

She had grabbed my hand, making me cross the threshold right behind her. I stepped in turn over the metal bar that marked the bottom of the narrow door. We were now inside the small space. We were now fully and yellowishly illuminated by the neon tube. We were now with our espadrilles brushing past the first circle of disassembled objects: twisted shafts and nails. The demobilizee moved and, once again, something tumbled from the summit of the scrap iron pile. It was an enamel coffeepot. The demobilizee let it roll into a nook with a sink and some toilets.

"And who is that someone?" he asked.

"My aunt," Rita Mirvrakis said boldly. "Daadza Bourbal."

The man paused, then cleared his throat.

"I once knew an Irma Bourbal," he said. "She used to live in the barracks on Albert Trott Street. Then she came here."

"That's my aunt," Rita Mirvrakis replied.

"She's dead," the soldier said. "It didn't go well for her. She had a place not far from here, two hundred meters away. It was a messy death."

"Oh," Rita Mirvrakis said.

"They captured her during an inspection," the demobilizee continued. "They accused her of being an Ybür. Are you an Ybür, little girl?"

"No," Rita Mirvrakis said.

"I am," I interrupted.

"They dragged her in the street behind their truck," the old man said. "She was a friend of mine. She passed right in front of the shop. It wasn't a pretty sight. I'm an Ybür, too."

In the middle of his amulets, medals, and lucky charms, there was a dangling string. It was wrapped around his neck. He grabbed it and revealed the sign that, until then, had remained hidden behind his back.

It is unknown what this creature is, or even if it is alive, the sign read. *Only an autopsy can establish these facts. Whoever you are, ensure the victory of scientific truth. Aid science. Kill this creature.*

Not without pride, I in turn exposed the cardboard rectangle that always swayed against my back, and whose contents were the same. There too, the brave were exhorted to shed light on scientific truth by taking adequate measures. *Dissect, dissect,* my cardboard advised. *Something will always come out of it.*

The demobilizee nodded his head approvingly.

"We were in a meeting hall, but we got chased out," Rita Mirvrakis said.

"You can stay here tonight," the old man proposed. "They've started dropping bombs again."

"We heard," Rita Mirvrakis said.

"It's dangerous to go out when they're dropping bombs," the old man warned.

"We know," Rita Mirvrakis said.

"What's your name?" the demobilizee asked.

"Rita Mirvrakis."

"And yours?"

"Imayo Özbeg."

"Good," the old man declared. "We're blood relatives."

He rose, took a cup from his pile, and left to fill it with tap water. Then he offered it to us. His amulets jingled as he walked. Some of them had bells. There were dozens of them. We swallowed a few mouthfuls. After our long walk through the city, our lips and tongues were completely dry.

"Want some more?" the soldier asked.

He looked at us wearily.

"Yes please," I said.

We drank a second cup. The container's rim smelled like motor oil, but we were thirsty.

We were intrigued by the charms. Few people wore them in the camp, except for exorcists and shamans, whom Granny Holgolde was always badmouthing. She accused them of practicing low magic and offending proletarian materialism and its fundamental values.

"Are you a shaman?" I asked.

"Um, well," the soldier replied.

"Do you do exorcisms?" Rita Mirvrakis asked.

"Of course not," the soldier protested. "But I can tell the future. People come to me for that, not to buy scrap metal . . . Imayo Özbeg, do you want me to read your fortune?"

"Yes, but do Rita Mirvrakis first," I proposed.

"No," she immediately refused. "We don't have time. We have to go."

However, she had sat on a crate after finishing the cup of water, and made no effort to get up.

She suddenly seemed odd. She had that look that sometimes deformed her face, before her pained sobs or delirious monologues.

"Go where?" the soldier asked.

My friend didn't respond. There was a silence. Outside, the street was empty. We heard a siren very far in the distance, several kilometers away. But that was all.

"Irma Bourbal," Rita Mirvrakis continued, "did she look like me?"

"No," said the soldier. "She was much taller than you. They tied her to the back of their truck with barbed wire and dragged her. When she passed by here, she already looked like nothing at all."

"I'm like her, anyway," Rita Mirvrakis muttered.

"It was raining," the soldier recounted. "Her body bounced through puddles. I had a hard time recognizing her, even though I knew it was her. Anyhow, she didn't look like you. She had a bad death."

"She looked like me," Rita Mirvrakis declared obstinately.

"No, she didn't," the soldier said.

He had an exhausted intonation and, after starting to make a gesture of denial, he frowned and remained silent for one, two minutes. Rita Mirvrakis lowered her head. She looked at who-knows-what, her eyes unmoving. I think she was already somewhere else, in her inner world, with her memories, her ghosts, and her terrible inventions.

I didn't know what would be best to do, so I remained standing in front of the demobilizee, planted on my heels, swaying as little as possible, like Soldier Schumann had taught us during our attention exercises.

From time to time, the neon tube crackled, but the light never changed. Despite the disorder and the shadows, the workshop's atmosphere was peaceful, though, obviously, somewhat strange, with these three persons who were together and unspeaking.

After a moment, the demobilizee came out of his sulk.

"So, do you want me to tell you your fortune, Imayo Özbeg?" he asked me.

I made a sign that meant yes.

The soldier made me sit beside him, on his car seat, and took my wrist in his coarse hand. We were pressed between two walls of junk, against lead tubes, dented wheels, rusted sluices, smashed electrical circuits, blackened lamps, twisted spoons and forks. From where I sat, I could see the iron shutter, and, beyond, the street with its leprosy of indistinctly glistening tar beneath the rays of a streetlight. The silhouettes of passersby were remarkable, though there wasn't enough time to determine to whom they belonged, or whether they were men or women. I didn't turn toward the soldier, who was speaking slowly and softly, as if half asleep and forever searching for ideas, images, and words. I breathed in the air filled with dust and metal shavings. I kept glancing at Rita Mirvrakis, hoping to catch her attention, watching for her complicity, but she didn't look at me. By my side, the soldier gave off a smell of burnt cardboard, of dirty clothing, of verdigris. It also occurred to me to close my eyes in order to better hear the phrases he pronounced, some of which, closer to mumbling than speech, escaped me.

It had been repeated to us a thousand times not to budge when an adult was talking to us, and I was immobile. But this immobility had another origin as well. Quite simply, his words petrified me. I felt as if the soldier, instead of amiably chatting about my future, was trying his best to instill me with fear. According to him, everything had gone bad right from the start and would continue to go bad right until the end.

No one had ever read my fortune before. I imagined that he was going to tell me about travels, encounters, mysterious astral conjunctions. I wasn't expecting anything particularly nice, but I was expecting something else.

"Whether you want it or not," the soldier said, "there is bad luck within you, Imayo Özbeg . . . it came with your birth . . . you were brought out of the darkness on a bad date . . . the very same day as the beginning of an ugly new war . . . you had to be pulled out with chains . . . you did your best not to emerge . . . you resisted, uselessly . . . misfortune also entered into your dreams at the same moment . . . and that, that will haunt you until your last breath . . . but even after that . . . it will follow you in your path to rebirth . . . there is no Clear Light for you in what is to come . . . in your fate, nothing will shine, except for unwanted flames, flames that bite and bring suffering . . . no other light on the path . . . Don't think you're the only one, if that is any comfort . . . For hominids and undermen of your kind, there is no exit or Clear Light . . . only a permanent feeling of failure . . . only the feeling of struggle without end, whether in dreams or in death . . . Sometimes it is as if you are struggling in a burning, tarry glue . . . no hope of even transforming at the last moment into a strange cormorant . . . wings unable to spread . . . bones dislocated from the effort to take flight . . . feathers gathered in a crumpled mass, stuck one to the other . . . breast faded . . . this is misfortune . . . orifices blocked by something neither solid nor liquid . . . breathing becoming more and more difficult . . . no more vertical, no more horizontal . . . a slanted, indeterminate bath, in an incomprehensible material . . . no more sides to reach or touch, nothing stable anywhere . . . a strange drowning . . . naphtha, oil . . . no recognizable sensation, no light . . . A struggle for nothing . . . When your turn comes, you will struggle in vain . . . if not in tar, then surrounded by flames . . . another misfortune . . . At first within the fire there are splendid colors . . . it is the heart of wonders . . . you are surrounded by orange scarves . . . profound shades that poets and painters claim to know how to describe . . . but they don't know what it all looks like from the inside . . . when you are inside the flames and burning . . . It's something else, another world . . . at first you think you've seen it before . . . then you make out other colors, terminal colors . . . fiery bronze, hellish yellow . . . smoky red, smoky crimson . . . and other colors still, with names unknown to the living . . . dark mochan . . . uldamor . . . camphormander . . . light mizerine, sparkling cynosure . . . mordant orange . . . If it's your turn in the flames, you'll struggle within, Imayo Özbeg . . . in vain . . . for animals, undermen, and humans, the outcome is always the same . . . you'll writhe in vain against adversity, in uldamor dispersal, in mizerine blindness . . . and then it will be all the same, you'll see . . . then you'll struggle in vain in the heart of death . . . even your rebirth won't happen . . . This is misfortune . . . You can't prepare for it, can't avoid it . . . Mordant orange at the end, but it's not the end . . . Imayo Özbeg, you will find refuge nowhere . . . Whether in life or in death . . . Your name burns . . . Your name will burn . . . Others will go to you, to your rescue or simply to accompany you, but even your name will burn . . . No one will be able to recognize you among the ashes . . . You will be nothing more than a strange cormorant in the depths of red . . . But what does anyone know about your future . . . no one knows anything about anything, we're already at the end of time . . . knowledge is worthless . . . preparation has no meaning . . . There's nothing but the flames to enter in death . . . There's nothing but dark tar and dark flames . . . Sometimes it's enough to set forth on the strange path of Bolshevism . . . it's enough to enter into that strange dream . . . Imayo Özbeg, you have this dream within you, as do we all . . . If your turn comes, you will struggle . . . you will try to put an end to misfortune . . . you will vainly try, when your turn comes, to put an end to misfortune . . . you will struggle between heaven and earth, in a squalid cluster of barbed wire . . . Achieving nothing . . . And then everything will be all the same . . . the blazing successes to start, the thousand-year-old victories, and almost immediately afterward the irreversible collapses, the defeats . . . the crushings . . . your bones and your intelligence will be ground into screams . . . at the final second you will contemplate your useless life, your fruitless death . . . your wounds . . . You have this dream within you like us all . . . you'll see . . . another form of misfortune that nothing can heal . . . And then . . ."

I had already heard enough. With an abrupt twist, I pulled back my hand. The soldier didn't try to take my wrist again; he shrugged and stopped talking. We were motionless, side by side, breathless, him from having spoken, me from having listened.

I felt like I had been beaten, or at least like I had been heavily and longly lectured for a sin I had not committed, but of which I was ashamed, despite everything, a sin inscribed within me since time immemorial, indelible and difficult to define.

I turned toward Rita Mirvrakis. I needed her protection, her false indifference, mean and affectionate. I needed to go to her and feel that we were together. Now she too gave the impression of having been beaten. She was curled up and trembling on the crate near the sink. Her eyes took in nothing of the exterior world. They looked glassy and mad.

"She's sick," I rasped.

"Who are you talking about?" the soldier asked, thinking about I don't know what.

"Rita Mirvrakis, I said. "She's sick."

The soldier looked in the girl's direction and, instantly, came out of his near-sleepwalking state. He jumped down from his seat and went to fill a cup of water and tried to make Rita Mirvrakis drink. Since she wouldn't part her lips, he put the container down, grabbed a piece of cloth, and, after moistening it under the spigot, returned to her. He began to softly wipe her pale face.

"Have you ever seen her in this state before?" he asked.

"Yes," I said. "She has episodes."

"It's filth from times past coming to the surface," the demobilizee said. "She, too, carries misfortune within her. It wells up from the past and spreads. It forms terrible images inside her skull and explodes. It destroys her interior. Maybe what I said brought it out. She took it for her own."

"Yes," I said, annoyed. "It's what you said that brought it out."

"She needs something sweet to counter the pain," the soldier sighed.

I scanned the room. Everything there was hard, blunt, and covered in grime. The soldier in turn looked around for something soft and caressing among the clutter and, finding nothing, became distraught and whined impotently. On the skin of his shaved head, between the close-cropped hairs, appeared tiny droplets of sweat. Rita Mirvrakis's episode pained him strongly, and his unease was transmitted to me, augmenting my own. I felt overwhelmed by fear. Out of sympathy for Rita Mirvrakis, I began to imagine the horrors that she was remembering or envisioning. Arrests, decapitations, screams, burnings. All of that mixed together with what the soldier had just evoked, with suffocation, with unknowable shades of red, with my own death in the middle of the flames.

"Go buy a jar of cream, Imayo Özbeg," the demobilizee proposed in a hoarse voice. "I have nothing for her here. The cream should do her some good."

"I don't have any money," I protested. "I don't know where the dairy store is."

"Tell the dairywoman that it's for the soldier Özbeg. She'll give me credit. Tell her that the soldier Özbeg says it's urgent."

"Your name's Özbeg too?" I asked, stunned.

"Yes, mine too. Like you. We're family."

"Oh," I commented, suspicious.

"That's how I know the details of your misfortune," the soldier explained.

"Granny Holgolde never told me about you," I remarked.

"Granny Holgolde doesn't have loose lips," the soldier approved. "In the camp, it's better not to show off one's relatives and genetic links."

I once again felt left in the dark. Out of everything in the world, I didn't understand the ways and secrets of adults the most.

"Genetic links, understand?" the soldier said.

"No," I said. "I don't understand anything you're saying."

The soldier Özbeg's skull shone beneath the neon light.

Rita Mirvrakis's state had not improved. There were bubbles of saliva at the corners of her lips. I went to touch her arm. She didn't react to my gesture. I felt the tension in her, the movement of frightening images, the collapse of her will in the face of such pain.

"Do you know where the dairy store is?" the soldier repeated.

"No," I said.

"Leave here and take a right. Go to the end of the street. There's a small landing with some stairs. You'll go down the steps. You can't miss it. At the bottom, turn left. There'll be a short street. The night is really dark. But there's always a light on above a doorway. You can use it to guide your way. It's the entrance to a barracks. Right next door is the dairy shop."

The soldier finished his description of the route.

"Did you get all that or do you want me to repeat it?" he asked.

"Landing, stairs, to the left a street with a light," I said. "That's not complicated. I won't get lost."

"Then go, Imayo Özbeg," the soldier said. "Go as fast as you can. Do you love Rita Mirvrakis?"

"Yes," I said in a breath.

"Then go quickly and come back just as quickly."

"What kind of cream?" I asked, suddenly panicked.

"A medium-sized one," the soldier clarified. "Like this."

He showed me the size with his hands. I nodded. He had already returned to Rita Mirvrakis. Once again he applied the damp rag to her forehead, her cheeks, her mouth, her wrists. Then he plucked off several of his charms and placed them on the little girl's stomach.

I rushed outside. The street was dark. Two sirens were blaring in the distance, clamoring in dismal variations. It wasn't raining, there was no fog, but the humidity in the air and the bituminous wind from the bomb that had just been dropped somewhere in the city were both palpable.

I barely crossed paths with anyone. For the first few hundred meters, I turned around every three steps to glance at the light from the workshop. It reassured and, in a certain way, spoke to me. There were other lamps sparking in the distance, but it was solely that one I tried to keep in my sight. I imagined the soldier stooped over Rita Mirvrakis, dampening her forehead, wiping her tears that didn't flow, shuffling around her, trying to calm her and ease her pain, her fears, whispering encouragements that she didn't want to listen to or couldn't hear. Then I started walking even faster. This portion of Vincents-Sanchaise Street was less shadowy, since it benefitted from the light of an ancient watchtower situated just behind a row of low houses. No one had scaled the tower's ladder in dozens of years, but there was still a working projector, doubtlessly fed by a special electrical grid. I ran past the tower and, five minutes later, found myself in front of the stairs the soldier had told me about. I went down them four at a time. Everything corresponded exactly to what he had described: the short street, the thick darkness, the orienting door lamp. I walked forward, taking precautions to keep myself from tripping. I regularly touched the wall to my right. The sirens were still blaring, but they sounded much farther away than when I was traversing Vincents-Sanchaise Street, and around me now I heard mainly the steady music of my own footsteps.

I reached the entrance to the barracks without incident. It looked abandoned or rarely used, more like a center for prisoners than a collective shelter. The gratings opened onto a long, deserted gallery. I could see doors on each side. They delineated the walls up to a second entryway that led to a dark courtyard or another street. Right in front of me, before the grate, extended a vast puddle of water whose depth was impossible to determine. On its bank lay a half-submerged canvas shoe.

I had no reason to dawdle and, after a moment, I continued walking. I crossed the last twenty meters and pushed open the glass door to the dairy shop.

The store was saturated with the smells of cheese and milk. I swallowed the nausea traveling up my throat and stepped up to the counter. My eyes were at the same height as the waxed cloth on which the dairywoman placed products for her clients and made change.

The shopkeeper was a large woman squeezed into a black dress adorned with little gray flowers, above which she had threaded a brown rubber pinafore that made her resemble a morgue worker. Her face was plump but her expression crabby, and she had pimples on her right cheek, which she had just been scratching and were bleeding. I immediately perceived her hostility. She leaned toward me, as if she was going to spit on or bite me.

"I'd like a jar of cream," I said.

"Do you have your container?" she asked.

Her voice was violent, resounding, with no attempt to sound friendly.

"I don't have a container," I said. "I came from the soldier Özbeg's."

"Bah, Özbeg," the dairy vendor commented. "He never pays what he owes, that one. He never returns his bottles. I've had it up to here with Özbeg. He can't have any cream without a container."

"It's an emergency," I said. "It's to save someone's life."

"So is it for him or is it not for him?"

"It's to save someone. Rita Mirvrakis."

"Is Rita your girlfriend?"

"Yes," I admitted with difficulty. "She needs something sweet to stop her pain."

"Did Özbeg tell you that?" the dairywoman asked.

"Yes."

"The stupidest things come out of that shaved head of his. He thinks he's a shaman. But he's nothing. I hear he wasn't even a good fighter. Those aren't medals on his chest, just bits of iron he found in the dump."

"He's taking care of Rita Mirvrakis," I said. "He's wiping away her tears. He needs some cream for Rita Mirvrakis. To take away her pain."

"You don't have a bottle," the dairy vendor persisted, making a face.

We stared at each other. I wouldn't show that I was afraid of her and that the smell of her store nauseated me. I continued hoping that she would ultimately yield. Behind her on a shelf were aligned several empty jars. I tried my best not to beg her to use one of those and to have pity for Rita Mirvrakis.

"What's your name?" she asked after a moment.

"Özbeg," I whispered. "I'm related to the soldier."

"Show me your sign."

I turned the sign that had been beating against my back around onto my chest.

If this individual does not undergo dissection, it said, *how can we know what its innards are like? Dissect, dissect. Something will always come out of it.*

"Oh," the dairywoman commented. "Even when you're dissected, you never know what your innards are like."

She shrugged, then turned toward the shelf that was drooping under the weight of plastic, glass, and tin jars. She examined them, her back turned to me. She had a plump back, with folds on the nape of her neck, as well as pimples and blotches around her head. I realized that she was going to fill one of those containers and give it to me after all. My heart began to beat faster, from both anxiety and gratitude.

"What kind of cream do you need?" she asked me, looking over her shoulder. "Sour, fresh, or skim?"

"I don't know," I said.

As we both hesitated, the ground trembled for a second. The windows and jars clinked.

"Well then," the dairywoman said.

There was a brief moment of stillness, then, once again, the earth trembled. Outside, we could hear an indistinct rumbling.

"It's bombs," the dairywoman said flatly.

I started counting in my head. If it really were bombs, two had already been dropped.

The almost total silence returned, then a neighborhood siren tore through the night: hoarse, sharp, and lacking in power. Then, there was another dull quake. Each time, all the glass jingled.

Three, I thought. Four.

The dairywoman, too, was counting. Her mouth was open, her brows were furrowed—she seemed more annoyed than frightened. After placing a translucent plastic jar on the counter, she unscrewed a large container of cream, but instead of scooping out one or two ladlefuls, she was busy scrutinizing the street.

"Four," she said.

I turned to look at what was happening on the other side of the shop's windows. I examined the exterior with her. Nothing could be seen. The beacon above the entrance to the barracks had just gone out. The darkness outside was impenetrable. The neighborhood siren sounded strangled. It made one last dull groan and then stopped. The window clinked once more, the ground rose. The lights inside the shop flickered.

Five, I thought.

The explosions were not particularly audible. They were more like a prolonged roll, like the passing of a distant line of tanks.

Then a man entered, out of breath and, skipping the customary greetings, he divulged what he knew. The war had started again, this time it was beginning with enormous, stationary bombs filled with bitumen. We had to leave quickly if we wanted to escape the pools of naphtha and gas. Vincents-Sanchaise Street had turned into hell.

"Twelve in all," he panted. "After the asphalt, they spit out gas. There can't have been any survivors."

"Twelve what?" the dairywoman interrupted.

"Twelve tons."

The man then quickly bounded outside and disappeared. He hadn't closed the door behind him, and suddenly from the street came the stench of burnt dust, of hot tar, of gasoline, of charred mattresses, of rubble. It was a terrifying smell. There was no smoke. It announced the approaching gas and was simply terrifying.

Now, in front of the store, there were people running in every direction. They were few in number, bent forward, and they were fleeing. No one had any sort of suitcase or bag. Aside from a few skeletal interjections, not a word was spoken. From time to time, the neighborhood siren struggled to emit another pathetic wail, but its gasps were short-lived. Above all else in the night was the sound of that continuous rumbling, which did not come from a line of tanks, but from the resulting combustion in the places bombarded. From the combustion, from the burial in progress, from drowning and asphyxiation in the bitumen.

I was in the middle of wondering whether I should still wait to be given some cream or if, on the contrary, I should get out of the shop and run as fast as I could back toward Vincents-Sanchaise Street, when from the back of the shop emerged a man wearing pajamas who had to be the dairywoman's husband. He walked with heavy steps toward his wife and placed his hand on the counter, his breathing labored. I think he was either very tired or very sick. Despite the time, he was half asleep. He was at least fifty and had the distraught face of a heart attack victim. The bags under his eyes were a sorry sight.

"What's going on?" he asked.

"They started bombing again," the woman said. "It's standing bombs this time. Vincents-Sanchaise Street is on fire. Once the asphalt cools a little, the gas is going to cover the entire city. It'll come on us from above. We won't escape."

"It's happening again," the man said, gasping for breath. "The extermination."

The dairywoman, seemingly mistrustful, sighed. She had hung her large spoon on a nail behind the counter. She closed the container from which she had meant to take a bit of cream.

"We need to get out of here," she said.

"Where can we go?" the man panted. "We'll be trapped by the gas. There's no place to run. Everywhere's the same."

"We'll go out the back," the dairywoman said. "Through the black space."

"The black space," the man repeated. "We don't even know where it goes to . . ."

"We have to go out the back," the woman insisted. "It's the only way."

"No one has ever come back," the man sputtered.

"You know how to open the door," the woman said. "It's either that or the gas."

"And the kid?" the man asked after glancing at me for a second. "What about the kid?"

"Are we taking him with us?"

"Are you serious?" the dairywoman protested. "First he wanted some cream for free, and didn't even have a container. Now you want us to bring him along too?"

The man couldn't catch his breath. He rattled like an over-stressed asthmatic.

"He doesn't look too bright," he finally said, fighting against the painful shuderrings of his lungs. "Out on the streets, with the bombs, he'll be lost."

"He's an Ybür," the woman said.

"What about internationalism?" the man protested.

"What about it?" the woman asked with irritation.

"You know very well," the man panted. "Proletarian . . . internationalism . . ."

The woman sucked her teeth contemptuously. "What a bunch of nonsense. You'd be better off taking off your pajamas and getting dressed."

The man grumbled.

"We were egalitarians, once," he remarked.

"Well, yes, but not anymore," the woman replied. "It's all screwed up now. That was the past."

"It'll come back," the man assured.

"Oh, it'll come back alright," the woman mocked. "After the bitumen."

They were obviously reviving an argument that had been going on between them for years. Worn out, discouraged, I observed their dialogue. I didn't know what to do. I wanted to dive out into the street and never see the two of them again. But I felt that, despite everything, and especially if they were leaving, I still had a small chance of getting the cream or maybe stealing a ladleful or two, and I remained glued in place in front of the counter, almost as if I were at attention, like an apprentice soldier waiting for orders that would never come. Rita Mirvrakis would have surely called me an idiot in that moment. The street behind me rustled. The inhabitants of the neighboring barracks were scattering, saying nothing as they ran, dressed like residents of a psychiatric asylum, in who knows what direction. There were no more explosions shaking the ground or the store's windows. All the sirens had died. Without the scraping and rush of steps, without the acrid smell of smoke, it would have almost been a normal night. I was waiting to find out whether the dairywoman and her husband were going to disappear or not, while, at the same time, thinking about Vincents-Sanchaise Street, the soldier Özbeg's workshop, and my friend Rita Mirvrakis.

"I'll take him out back too," the woman finally decided.

"Good," the man approved.

"I'm only doing it to make you happy," the woman said. "But once we get there, that's it. We're not bringing him with us."

"Then he'll need a light," the man wheezed. "Out back, the darkness is too dark."

"Go get dressed," the woman said. "You know well and good that out there we can't have any lights. Put our things in a bag with two bottles of milk. I'm coming."

The man returned to the back room.

"Did you hear that?" the dairywoman asked.

"No," I lied.

"You don't have to go back to Vincents-Sanchaise Street."

"But they're waiting for me," I said. "I have to go back. It's an emergency."

"There's nothing there anymore," the dairywoman said. "There's no more street. They're quiet bombs. They don't make any noise but they turn everything to ash. They explode silently, houses crumble, people drown in a sticky paste. Then the gas spreads. It eliminates everything still breathing."

"Rita Mirvrakis is waiting for me," I said.

I tried to hold back my tears, but they were already beginning to blur my vision.

"She's not there anymore," the dairywoman said with a horrible rictus, out of either compassion or discomfort. "She's nowhere anymore."

"Where is she?" I started to panic.

"Idiot," the dairywoman said. "You know very well."

The tears welled up under my eyelids. I raised my head so as not to produce an obscene sniffling sound. I was ashamed of crying in front of someone I didn't know, in front of someone other than Rita Mirvrakis.

"No, I have to go look for her," I said. "We're together."

"You won't find her," the dairywoman reasoned with me. "It's all over for her. For the soldier Özbeg too. Now, you have to go out back."

"Where does it go?"

"I don't know. No one I know of has ever been. Once we go through, we can't come back. No one has ever come back. But it seems like our only chance to live."

"I don't care about living," I sobbed. "I want to bring Rita Mirvrakis some cream. She needs it. Otherwise, she could die."

"You're never going to see your fiancée again," the dairywoman explained once more. "It's over for her. She doesn't need cream or anything else anymore."

"No, she still needs it," I sobbed.

Through the door now came puffs of awful-smelling smoke. The street was empty once more. There had not been many boarders in the barracks, and everyone still alive had already fled. The smoke was suddenly visible, a velvety gray that made me want to vomit, and it carried with it memories of charred clothing, rooms drowned in tar, bodies braced in vain against the agony of the fire.

A lamp above the creamery went out. The others were flickering. The light continued to dim. The back room had been plunged into darkness.

"We have to hurry," the dairywoman said.

She walked around the counter and approached me, then took me by the hand. I resisted for a moment, on principle, but I didn't have it in me for long. This woman was commanding and powerful. Few adults had taken my hand these past years. With Rita Mirvrakis, I associated the gesture with loving tenderness, but, coming from adults, I saw only punishment or unpleasant obligation. Back at the meeting hall, the nurses and aunts rarely touched us, only for reprimands and medical examinations. When we went to the canteen or showers, the supervisors might push us to make us hurry along, but that was always accompanied by a furious exclamation or a glare. They never held the hands of boys or girls older than four or five.

The dairywoman pulled me behind her as we came into an intermediary room that had not yet been overwhelmed by the fumes from outside and which smelled of rancid butter, whey, and rotten vegetables. It was also very dark. Without letting go of me, the dairywoman passed by a row of shelves full of ripening cheeses and knocked on a small door. Almost immediately, as if he had been standing on the other side and awaiting this signal, her husband opened it. Over his pajamas, he had slipped on a pullover full of holes and a coat that he had left unbuttoned and which went down to his ankles. He handed his wife some clothing of the same type, an enormous green raincoat she immediately put on without a word. He was carrying on a strap a shapeless bag. He was out of breath, and panic glistened in his exhausted eyes.

"Did you get the milk?" the dairywoman asked.

"Yes, three bottles," the man said.

"The good stuff?"

"Top shelf."

"And the pemmican?"

"All that was left."

"Good," the woman said. "Turn off the lights. We're leaving right now."

"What about him?" the man asked.

"He's coming with us, like I told you," the woman answered impatiently.

The man went back into the shop, lowered the front grate, and switched off the circuit breaker. Darkness surrounded us. I then heard the man grope around as he approached us. His steps weren't even and, when he reached the level of the shelves, he stumbled on a hurdle and protested. With a plopping, animalistic, almost tranquil sound, several creamy masses crashed onto the ground.

"I knocked over some of the cheeses," he apologized.

"Who cares?" the dairywoman replied. "We're not coming back. The cheeses are done for anyway."

"Oh," the man wheezed. "Well, I'm walking in it."

"Go open the door," the woman said.

The man passed by us and began fumbling with a wall in which, when there was still light, I hadn't seen any opening. We could hear his distressed, labored breathing.

"They've gotten rid of the airlocks," he grumbled.

"Open it anyway," the woman said.

"It's going to blow," the man warned.

"What can you do," the dairywoman replied.

Her husband struggled with latches and bars, and maybe also with a valve that at first was stuck in place, but then began to creak with each quarter turn. After a minute, something came loose, a metallic object banged against the ground. There was the sound of whining hinges.

"Don't move," the man warned.

There was an inhaling sound. Suddenly, a lukewarm breeze from the other side covered me in a thin layer of dust. I continued to cry silently and, from time to time, rubbed my eyelids with the hand that wasn't imprisoned in the dairywoman's. The wind made my fingers begin to smell like charcoal, underground substances, and mouse urine. Then, the wind stopped. I supposed the problems due to the absence of an airlock were now resolved.

The dairywoman pulled me behind her into the dark and we crossed the threshold of that strange door, which for the two adults symbolized a permanent farewell to cream production and small business ownership, and for me a farewell to the city in flames and the one I loved, and for us all, a farewell to existence as we knew it.

I began walking alongside my guide. The ground made a squeaking sound as we treaded over it, as if it were made of scoria. The dairywoman's husband had closed the door behind us before catching up. No one could see a thing. We had left the city and its flashes and rumbles of war. I think we were moving through a tunnel, but there weren't any echoes, and we seemed to be out in open air, in a place where the sky, for one reason or another, had disappeared. Nothing could be confirmed. There was no sound other than that of our feet pressing against the ground's friable surface. The temperature was mild, the humidity agreeable. The two adults didn't speak a word. The dairywoman's husband was having trouble breathing and, every fifty meters, would stop to wheeze and express a violent pain. Without commentary, the dairywoman would stop too, and, hand in hand, we would wait for the straggler. Then the woman let go of me. She knew that, now, I had accompanied them too far for me to flee, too far into the darkness and too far into the incomprehensible and the unknown.

We moved blindly, slowly, bending toward the shadows as one bends toward an adverse wind. We tried our best not to waver or collide with each other and, when it did happen, we felt discomfort and quickly backed away, as if we had been burned, or, in any case, as if we wanted to bring an end to an obscene situation.

Around midnight, a man suddenly appeared on our left and began walking with us, without exchanging a word with the dairywoman or her husband; I couldn't tell whether he was someone familiar to them or someone unwelcome. I listened to the ground crinkle beneath his feet and, occasionally, the clearing of his throat and his breathing. He too was short-winded. He kept pace with us, but at the same time, he always stayed a few meters away from our group, so as not to stumble into one of us by accident. I had the impression that neither the dairywoman nor her husband were aware of his presence, or at least that they tolerated him with no regard, as if he were simply a wandering dog that decided to follow them, wanting neither food nor pets. When the dairywoman's husband stopped to breathe, our traveling companion continued walking for a dozen or so steps, then stopped in turn, waiting, like us, for the invalid to find a bearable pulmonary rhythm and catch up to us.

We continued like this for an hour or two more, then the dairywoman decreed that it was time to rest for a moment. We had no more strength. The unknown man froze nearby. The light all around us was almost nonexistent, like in the ocean's abyssal zones. Nothing broke the silence after we stopped treading the ground, covered in ash, scoria, or some other friable material. On the other side of the seal, we had crossed into a different world. Total darkness, monotony, bleak odors—all served as scenery in an aimless march and indecisive rumination on current events, past lives, and those whom we had left behind forever. I couldn't help but think about the place after death the soldier Schumann would talk about, repeating the lessons of his Buddhist comrades in the barracks. I also remembered Granny Holgolde's tales, the tunnels and black deserts that the elephant Ashkarot traversed whenever she changed existences and homes. We were in a world of that type. The difference perhaps was that we were crossing it together instead of being forced to confront a frightening solitude.

All three of us sat on the ground. The dairywoman's husband opened his bag and took out a bottle of milk. He handed it to the dairywoman. I heard a swallowing sound. He in turn quenched his thirst.

Then he sought out my hands and invited me to close my fingers around the glass container.

"Don't drink more than a mouthful," he advised. "It's condensed."

"It has pemmican in it," the dairywoman added.

I swallowed two gulps. The liquid was grainy and tasted like meat, but it comforted me. After drinking, I wiped my lips and gave the bottle back to him.

"We can survive a few weeks more on that," the husband said.

"Of course," the dairywoman commented.

We remained seated for a moment, saying nothing. We were in a row, facing the vast nothing, our eyes taking in the total absence of image and light, unable to distinguish between the top and bottom of the shadows. There may have been an immense vault above us, or a sky, and before us an endless black plain, or walls. We saw nothing. Beneath us, the ground was neither cold nor hot. Our bodies were now very close to one another, and I wasn't disturbed at all by the dairywoman's heat, even though not long ago, when we were walking, the slightest brush from her side or her hand filled me with shame. I listened to her husband's wheezing inhalations, the sounds coming from her stomach.

Several meters away from us, our traveling companion had finally settled on the ground. I didn't know whether he was slouched or squatting or even sitting like us, but I heard him fill and empty his lungs in an irregular, convulsive manner. It was impossible to guess if he was saddened not to be invited to share in our meal or if he didn't care at all.

"You know, Özbeg," the dairywoman said suddenly, "we have less than a one-in-a-hundred chance of getting out of here. It was that or the gas. At any rate, if you'd gone back, you'd be dead right now. You probably would have put up a fight on Vincents-Sanchaise

Street, but you wouldn't have lasted. You'd reach the top of the stairs and get buried in tar. By the time you opened your mouth to scream, you'd already be swallowed up by the flames. You wouldn't have been able to find your little fiancée, Milvamakis."

I cut in.

"Rita Mirvrakis," I corrected.

My voice was distorted by a sob. I hadn't been able to cry for hours, but occasionally I felt a spasm of despair seize my rib cage.

"You wouldn't even have been able to see her," the dairywoman continued. "You would've been trapped in the bitumen right from the start. You'd sink in it to your knees, then to your chest, with nothing below you to keep you upright. The flames would've lapped you up. You would've tried to breathe, but you'd only breathe in the gas. You wouldn't have even had the time to open your mouth to call Rifka Marvrakis by her name."

"Rita Mirvrakis," I said.

"That's what I mean," she continued. "You would've just breathed in toxic gas. Then you'd be dead. Your body would've turned into something like liquid soot. You'd have been stuck in the tar head-first. It would've swallowed you up. Your head would be a piece of black cheese. The flames would've lapped you up again. Then it would've all been over."

"Don't say that," the dairywoman's husband exhaled violently.

"Why?" she protested. "Aren't I right?"

"You still shouldn't say it. It's scaring him."

I heard a coat rustle. The dairywoman turned to face me.

"Are you scared, Özbeg?" she asked.

"No," I lied.

Thus ended our conversation.

We didn't even think about getting up. We stayed there, neither moving nor speaking, for a length of time I can't evaluate with any precision, at first several hours, but then, since the nights had no end and came with no change in temperature or light, in all likelihood a day or two, or a short week. I felt numb, but didn't want to sleep. I thought of my past life, of the school hall, of Rita Mirvrakis, of my barrackmates, of the soldier Schumann, of Granny Holgolde and other adults. The images turned slowly inside my head. I listened to the sounds produced at my side by the bodies of the dairywoman and her husband, the labored breathing of the stranger camping with us here in the dark. There existed no other way to measure the time. The gurglings emitted by the dairywoman's mouth, stomach, and intestines, the flatulences, the whistling emitted from the lungs of first one adult, then the other—these are what gave rhythm to the night. From time to time as well, the dairywoman would get up to relieve herself at a distance. For some reason, only she was concerned with this need. It was an expedition made without discretion, since she feared not being able to find her way back, and so never strayed far. We followed her movements with our ears, and I even had the impression that the two men, the husband and our unknown traveling companion, were holding their breath for the entire duration of the event. I was also curious about what was happening and, orienting my face toward where she was squatting, I tried to imagine precisely the different phases of the operation. Then she would come back to us and, often, her husband would take advantage of the occasion to decree a lunch break, as if all three of us had just carried out a considerable task, following which our bodies required nourishment posthaste. He would uncork the same bottle of milk and pass it around. Once more, I would swallow a mouthful or two of the pemmican-infused liquid in silence, with the feeling that I had thus prolonged my survival by at least one more night. Then everything from before would resume, the monotony of the hours, the monotony of the bodily murmurs, and the monotony of the absolute darkness.

Much later, an incident disrupted this routine.

While on one of her excremental adventures, the dairywoman happened to miscalculate her return trajectory and lost her way. I heard her stand up after urinating, to the right of where I was sitting, about fifteen meters or so away. She adjusted her clothes and began walking, her footsteps heavy, causing the ashy ground below her to squeak. At first I thought she had mixed up her directions, but we had fallen into the habit of remaining practically mute, exchanging no words at all with one another, so I felt it would be too bizarre for me to call out to her. I also thought she would quickly correct herself. But then, after passing by us at eye level, she veered off and, turning toward the stranger's campsite, headed into the distance. She stopped, listened, took two steps in one direction, listened, shuffled her feet, then bravely took a dozen more steps, then stopped again. Everyone could perceive her hesitation, anguished and anguishing in its form. I was going to signal our presence to her with some kind of shout, but I had no idea what to say. I didn't know her name and, as I was reflecting on what to yell, the dairywoman's husband grabbed my arm and squeezed it lightly. I understood that he was forbidding me from making any kind of sound.

"She's going to get lost," I whispered.

"You can't raise your voice," he breathed. "Not for any reason."

"Why?" I asked.

"We don't shout here," he said.

"But she won't be able to get back," I said.

At that moment, I heard the man who, up to then, had been resting nearby, get up and begin to walk. He was following her. Their steps now seemed synchronized. They couldn't be more than twenty meters apart from each other.

"That man's walking behind her," I whispered.

I don't know whether he was following or chasing her. But he was walking behind her and, according to the noises, it seemed that he was catching up to her little by little. Already the sounds had diminished, as the increasing distance made them less and less audible, but that's how it seemed. I shivered. I thought of a falcon inexorably approaching its prey.

"He's going to catch her," I whispered.

"Yes," the husband rasped. "He thinks she has the milk."

I heard him grope around and then gasp. He was looking for his bag but couldn't find it.

"Well," he finally said. "She took the milk. I didn't hear a thing. Neither of us did. She ran off with the milk."

I didn't really care, but I gasped slightly as well.

"She ran off with the milk and that guy," the dairywoman's husband said.

"Oh," I commented.

For two or three minutes, the steps echoed in the crushing silence of the night, then they faded away completely and forever.

Several hours more went by. We were sitting side by side, the dairywoman's husband and I, looking straight ahead, seeing nothing. He said nothing more about the milk his wife had pilfered. He was having enormous trouble breathing and seemed primarily occupied by his final moments.

"Meeting in basement thirty-six," he suddenly roared.

Then I heard him collapse. He was no longer breathing.

I stayed there for a long time without reacting. Then I stretched out my hand to touch the corpse beside me. There was neither anything nor anyone.

I knew then that I was dreaming, and felt relieved.

I only have to wait for the end of the night, I thought. I'm going to wake up. I'll open my eyes and once more see everything real around me. I only have to calmly wait for that reappearance, I thought. It's going to come, sooner or later.

The ground's warmth invited me to lay down, so I made myself comfortable, my arms crossed behind my head. I thought about everyone I was going to see again, my barrackmates, the guards, our aunts, Granny Holgolde, the soldiers in the hall, the invalids, the demobilizees, the insane.

And, of course, I thought about you, Rita Mirvrakis. I was going toward you. I knew there was nothing more to do but to wait.

I'm still waiting. But I was moving toward you and, in this moment still, I am moving toward you, Rita Mirvrakis, I am moving toward you.

Granny Holgolde's Tale: The Abyss

The rain had stopped a good twenty minutes ago, but the humidity was still dripping onto the leaves of banana trees, giant rhubarbs, monstrous philodendrons, and, when she stopped walking, Marta Ashkarot listened to the nocturnal silence and delighted in its music, at once monotonous and irregular. It was a very hot hour of the night. The forest was drowned in a torrid mist. Clouds floated at a low altitude, exaggerating the sense of heavy dampness and obscuring the starlight. The elephant advanced carefully on the deserted route, an old trail that had been largely swallowed up by the surrounding vegetation, but which also, at key points, had conserved its nature as a path created by professional clearers, and which had remained practically unchanged since the time when humans were the dominant species.

Marta Ashkarot walked slowly. Under more normal atmospheric conditions, she would have noticed residual glimmers even on dark, starless nights, but, this day, the blackness of the sky was joined by the opacity of the fog, and she could see nothing. This did not stop her from tranquilly pushing ahead, however. She didn't pay too much mind to the mudholes, puddles, and bogs whose presence she would surmise just before sinking up to her knees. When a fallen log barred the path, she would detect the obstacle with her trunk and step over it. Sometimes she would wind up startling a family of tree frogs or a cane toad, and sometimes she would hear a large grass snake hastily slither away so as not to be trampled beneath her feet, but this was far from a common occurrence. The forest was devoid of beasts, not to mention hominids and monkeys, which she never came across anymore. In the semiaquatic world, like everywhere else, life had made itself scarce.

All around her, silence reigned.

Her eyes provided her with no information, and in order to guide herself she had to rely on her senses of smell and hearing. She progressed this way, ears deployed and trunk on alert, as she dexterously pranced about, often slowing to take in the night. She felt dripping sweat, mud, and plant sap all over her body. She didn't forbid herself from sleeping, from time to time. She would ensconce herself within a thicket, preferably beneath a ceriman or a carambola, so she could chew on the tree's fruits while she napped. That kept her well rested so she could continue forward on her blind march.

She had traveled a kilometer since her last break, when suddenly she felt a current of air. There was a breeze blowing against her forehead and feet. It produced a very faint whistle and lowered the temperature at least three or four degrees. The air was moving from right to left, and seemed to cross the path. Well, what's this? she thought. Nothing could explain such a phenomenon. She quickly came to a halt in order to explore the darkness and find out more. She swung her trunk forward and around her flanks, sniffed intensely, and thought. She repeated these operations for an entire minute. All her observations concurred: there was no more vegetation ahead of her, no more trail, no more trees. There was only sky and fog. As strange as it seemed, the path abruptly stopped. It ended sharply at a ravine or abyss. Instead of falling into a pothole, or sinking into a quagmire or puddle, a normal occurrence in a forest, quite simply she was at the brink of a fatal plunge over an unknown precipice.

On contemplation, a shiver of both vertigo and fear ran through her. She couldn't be certain of the depth of the chasm before her, but it was in fact a chasm. The coolness of the air and absence of any echo made clear that she was now in the presence of a prodigious void.

The elephant took a step back. She was not very delicate, in general, but in this case, she had measured the risk and faltered.

"Well," she muttered. "One more step and you'd wind up in a thousand pieces at the bottom of a ravine, old Marta!"

Gosh, she thought. Almost three hundred meters, I bet. There I was on my merry way and now here I am. I would've gotten it good! I'd have been marmalade right about now! Paste!

"Good thing you stopped in time, old girl!" she whispered under her breath.

Her heart was pounding. A foul, animalistic sweat pooled beneath her breast, and, spurred by emotion, she hadn't been able to avoid letting out a small burst of urine between her hind feet.

Well, that's enough of that, she thought. I'll wait for morning and won't move an inch until then.

Her journey that night had come to an end.

You shouldn't always rush blindly ahead, she thought to finish.

She sat down, her four feet, still trembling, planted on the ground. Then her enormous muscles relaxed, as the images that had provoked her surprise urination began to fade. One after the other, the dark visions of her death lost their dreadful realism. Her carcass broken on the pebbles and scree, her skull in a thousand pieces, her limbs twisted into intolerable positions. Little by little, she forgot her fear.

For four or five hours, there wasn't a sound, save for the blowing of the wind that indicated the gap's presence, and, from time to time, the ringing of drops on the leaves of giant fig trees and in the forest's puddles.

The singing of the wind. The singing of water on leaves. The impenetrable dark.

The hours passed.

The shadows were covered in a padded blanket of fog.

Marta Ashkarot slept.

Then, although nothing interrupted the night, she heard footsteps. Footsteps! Coming down the path was a bipedal creature endowed with shoes, and thus related to hominids or something like them. The creature was walking, it seemed, at a brisk pace, without taking any particular precautions. It strode boldly through the darkness, indifferent to obstacles, piles of leaves, or sludgy mires. Its rhythm was steady, and Marta Ashkarot imagined it swinging its arms with enthusiasm, rather than holding them ahead in order to defend itself against any surprises in the night.

A soldier, the elephant thought. It might be an infantryman, and one who's got some guts, too.

Two hundred meters separated them, then the distance quickly reduced, and the figure was right beside Marta Ashkarot. It advanced like a precise mechanism. It brushed past the elephant without seeing her and, without any aggression, continued on its way. It went straight toward the abyss. Marta Ashkarot stretched out her trunk and pulled it back at the last second. The stranger shouted in surprise and fear, a sharp, piercing shout. It seemed this intrepid walker was a woman.

"You were going to fall into the ravine," the elephant said.

"What ravine?" the woman asked.

"The path stops up ahead," the elephant explained. "There's a hole. You can't see a thing. It'd be better to wait for dawn and find a different route."

She still had the end of her trunk solidly curled over the shoulder of her interlocutor and felt her begin to relax. At first, the woman hadn't understood what was happening, and doubtlessly thought it was an attack, but, now, she was calming down.

"Let me go," she said.

Marta Ashkarot withdrew her trunk back to her mouth and stepped a meter away.

The woman went to feel out the place where the path ended and whistled through her teeth.

"It seems deep," she admitted.

"See?" the elephant said.

They agreed to wait for the morning together and took advantage of the situation to have a peaceful talk. The woman's name was Irina Wu. She was fifty-seven years old. She wanted to join a revolutionary unit whose existence she had learned of in her youth, the Red Women's Detachment.

"That's just an old legend," the elephant said. "No one's been in this region for ages. No more revolutionaries, no more heroic resistance fighters, no more of anything."

"Don't be a defeatist," Irina Wu said. "In the past, we used to put defeatists up against the wall."

"There aren't any walls anymore either," the elephant remarked.

"If that's the case, we'll build them again," Irina Wu promised.

She belonged to a species of impertinent optimists. Marta Ashkarot did not share her voluntaristic euphoria and inserted here and there several cooling objections, but she carefully considered her words. She envied this woman's capacity for rejecting catastrophe, for downplaying all its aspects, and for considering a negative tone to be tantamount to betraying the Party, to denying the Party's traditions and theorists, and especially to shoving aside the thousands of humans who had once placed their hope in egalitarianism. That there were no more survivors to contemplate the disaster did not deflate Irina Wu's spirit, and, as the elephant did not hold to dealing with truisms and arguments like an old sectarian, she didn't make any effort to contradict her. The two conversed amicably, without polemicizing, as comrades. Thus they reached morning.

The fog cleared with the night, and when the light of dawn finally broke, both Irina Wu and Marta Ashkarot crept forward to where the path disappeared, in order to get a look at their surroundings.

It was a vision so astounding, so beautiful, that the two let a long—a very long—moment go by without uttering a word. It was as though they were completely paralyzed.

They were at the edge of a spectacular crevice, a geological accident that must have affected the entire continental shelf and was responsible for the appearance of an immense cliff. The earth had collapsed along an extraordinarily straight and brutal line, which now stretched without interruption from east to west, from mist to mist, dividing the earth into two horizontal worlds, separated and mirrored, into two lands covered in dense and fluffy vegetation, in emerald green, soft green, old green, foggy green, rubber plant green, banana tree green, from which here and there emerged impossibly tall, vine-covered trees with neither name nor form, which in a distant time or place would have played host to hordes of chattering monkeys. The cliff was about eighty meters tall and quite steep. With the right equipment, alpinists may have been able to risk a descent. But, for ordinary travelers, it offered no possibility of crossing. You would have to either turn around, or walk alongside the void for days, perhaps weeks, searching for a place less abrupt.

"It's like the waterfalls of the Zambezi, but without any water," Marta Ashkarot observed.

"You've been to the Zambezi?" Irina Wu asked in amazement.

"No," the elephant said. "But I've heard of it."

The two were filled with emotion in the face of this gigantic rift in the earth, this forest extending over two levels, and which, now that it was lit by the light of the heavy, equatorial, sunless sky, was witness to the immensity of the world, its admirable serenity.

Irina Wu was dressed like anyone who desired to join a red women's detachment: an infantry outfit made of long-lasting hessian, though worn thin from numerous washings and years of wandering, pants that didn't cling to the legs, solid espadrilles, a cap adorned with a red star. She wore across her stomach a small bag containing a bit of cloth, basic toiletries, a thermos, and survival gear. She was crouching at the edge of the precipice.

"Be careful not to fall, dear," the elephant said with concern.

Irina Wu made a vague gesture. She seemed to be struggling with emotion more than vertigo, and didn't wish to flaunt these sentiments. Marta Ashkarot noticed the tears in her eyes.

They remained for another hour side by side, facing the void, facing the sky and the green world, unmoving and beyond compare.

"It's magnificent," Irina Wu finally said.

"Yes," Marta Ashkarot agreed. "It's magnificent."

Irina Wu stretched her hand downward and toward the horizon.

"We're in a place with practically infinite resources," she said. "There's all the water and wood we could want. The climate is ideal. We can rebuild everything, recreate cities, industrialize."

"Bah," the elephant objected.

"We'll divide production between all the workers. We'll establish a classless society."

"Bah," the elephant objected once more. "We'd need at least a few more people for that."

Irina Wu nodded her head.

"Well, I know that's a problem," Irina Wu admitted. "I don't have my head buried in the sand. You're right. For this to really take flight, we'd need at least a few more."

My Parents

1.

For a wide decade of the last century, Granny Holgolde was the director of a service that managed the reinsertion of assassins of important enemies and mercenaries, and, as a middle manager, contributed generously to the persistence of the underground vanguard, to the clandestine progression of revolutionary currents, and to the promise that one day, at the global level, the mutinies would begin anew. Those under Granny Holgolde's protection escaped the police for good. They became nameless and insignificant, working modest and diverse jobs, sometimes as employees in inconsequential administrations, sometimes in food companies, or otherwise as public writers on the outskirts of the camps, but sometimes they were given missions as well, and would then once more lend a hand to lost clandestines or shadowy militants, or assist asylum escapees, to outcasts like us, tempted by an immediate and radical communism, at odds with the mechanisms of public morality.

My father had benefited from Granny Holgolde's special aid, and, the year he met my mother, he was managing a tiny workshop that repaired household objects such as hairdryers, radiocassettes, and bicycles. The workshop had an agreement with a neighboring factory, which provided it with brass wire, threaded rods, and metal scraps that my father worked and transformed into spare parts.

One day, my mother, who was working as a sweeper in the mechanics' workshops, was tasked with transporting a crate from one place to another.

She had placed the crate on her delivery tricycle's trailer, and, while pedaling dreamily along the Kanal, already in sight of the warehouse where my father was stationed, she was attacked by Werschwell Fraction activists. Since she hadn't turned around in time and could no longer flee, my mother defended herself. My grandmothers had taught her how to fight. However, she was no match against two quadragenarians well-trained in genetic cleansing and humanitarian operations in the ghettos. She had first tried to dissuade them from touching her, opposing their vulgar remarks with a disquieting indifference, but this kind of subtlety almost never works on brutish types, and, when physical confrontation became inevitable, she wounded the skinnier of the two with a blade to the face. The man was bleeding and shouting as if she had slit his throat when his companion, at first stunned by this Ybür woman facing them down, started to move toward her. The blood and pain had heightened their fury. My mother then knew that all was lost.

It was here that my father intervened. In the time before he had become Granny Holgolde's protégé, he too had learned how to fight, but from instructors who were not stage fighters, and whose techniques all had as their objective the death of one's adversary. He ran toward the Kanal and, in less than half a minute, caught up with the trio, obviously in order to stand up for the woman in danger. He was a swift and efficient man. First he broke the skinny one's spinal column with a blow to the neck. Then he jabbed an enormous spike twice into the other one's temple. Versions vary with the telling, and sometimes it's a carpenter's nail, while other times a screwdriver. Regardless, he jabbed the object into the other one's temple.

It was just after, next to these bodies, surrounded by heaps of scrap metal, that my mother and father met.

2.

My mother was pedaling along the Kanal, towing behind her a crate haphazardly filled with iron scraps, copper tubes, threaded rods, wingnuts, and all sorts of electrical castoffs. She had been entrusted with these things at the factory. The courier who was ordinarily in charge of this miserable route was absent, and, since she had finished her cleaning duties, she had been asked to take his place. She was to bring her cargo to a maker who worked in a small repair shop, where these bits of garbage would become useful tools, living pieces, thanks to which broken machines would work once more. I believe the crate was heavy, and that my mother, on her tricycle, had to make an effort to keep going, weaving, perhaps, across the Kanal's deserted quay.

The weather was a little cold, as this was in October. The cloudy, poorly lit sky loomed over the landscape. Camp 801 in this place was composed mainly of abandoned construction sites and houses whose windows were sealed with bricks or planks, or which were demolished. Some were closed off with barbed wire. From the corner of her eye, beyond the railing, my mother caught the image of stagnant, dark green waters, dirtied here and there by a gray film of pollution. On her right, apart from the crumbling houses, she passed by fences on which had been pasted propaganda posters, with portraits of leaders or deputies, which she ignored, which deserved nothing but sputum, and to which she didn't spare the slightest thought. Protesters had scratched injurious comments over them. The ink on the aging paper had faded. The commenters must have been killed, maimed, or sent to solitary confinement a long time ago.

My mother attempted to decipher the worn, hastily scrawled phrases, made under the influence of powerless indignation and fear. She meditated on what she herself would have written. In any case, her attention was distracted, and she was slow to notice the two men who seemed to be in the middle of a conversation on the quay, in front of a gray, dead house that looked to have once been home to a restaurant or bar. They were standing next to a door that was vaguely condemned by a square of sheet metal. She wondered who they were waiting for. She continued pedaling in their direction. They were planted there like dumb statues, staring at that decrepit restaurant. Perhaps they had wanted to go inside, warm up, and drink a beer. Or perhaps this place had been chosen by them as a meeting point for another person who hadn't arrived yet. Or perhaps they were waiting for someone to come out of the abandoned building and join them. They were standing there and they were smoking.

Then, though it was too late for her to turn back, she saw that they were wearing Werschwell Fraction armbands. Two short-haired quadragenarians in brown leather jackets, surrounded by an aura of malevolence. She was already in the pogromists' twisted sight. A stocky boar and his associate, who was an entire head taller. One heavy brute with a dauntless appearance, and one irritable. Two dangerous animals.

They suddenly came to life, letting out one last breath and throwing their still-lit cigarettes onto the ground.

It wasn't my mother in particular that they were waiting for, but, since she was there, they decided to give her what she had coming. My mother was an Ybür, and this was obvious; my mother was a worker, and thus potentially sympathetic to egalitarians and subversives, and this was obvious.

The two Werschwell Fraction soldiers moved almost lethargically as they placed themselves in the middle of the path. My mother stopped. The taller and skinnier of the two men walked toward my mother and grabbed her tricycle's handlebars.

The landscape was gray and unwelcoming. At the end of the quay, the Kanal sunk beneath a vault, then curved to the west. The street where my father worked began there, less than a hundred meters away. The entire area looked uninhabited. The repair shop was open, and my mother had the impression that someone there was stooped over a workbench, but everywhere else, there was nothing and no one.

There was nothing and no one, and the image suddenly seemed frozen, hopeless, consisting of only this Ybür woman and the two armband-wearing quadragenarians facing her, in the morning's silent monotones, beside the dirty green water of the Kanal.

3.

My father was in the middle of dismantling a refrigerator motor when he saw, a hundred meters away from his workshop, on the Kanal quay, something resembling a silent quarrel. Two brutes were bothering a young woman as she stared them down.

My father abandoned his workbench, walked to the doorway of his miniscule shop, and squinted. Although he didn't wear glasses yet, his vision back then was already deficient. However, he could see enough to notice around the men's arms the ribbon of crimson, burgundy, and purple with which the defenders of order adorned their flags and liturgical pieces. He then grabbed a screwdriver and ran toward the small gathering.

The two men hadn't seen him approach and, once he was close to them, he realized they were in a state of growling, quasi-animal rage. At the very start of the hostilities, the young woman had been able to turn back to the trailer and pick up a metal triangle from the crate. She had used it as a razor to slash the tall skinny one's face, the closer of her two aggressors. She was right to do such, she had no other choice, and her hand hadn't trembled. Any one of us would have done the same thing. But the result of this action was to drag her adversaries into a violence certainly less hesitant than when they had merely blocked her way. The one with the body of a wrestler had walked up to her, disarmed her with a smack, then pulled her from the bike on which she had been keeping her balance, and, in the same moment, threw her onto the ground to give her a thrashing. His skinnier companion was shouting spasmodic and whining protests. He was kept bringing his hands to the wound and then hysterically examining the blood. My father felt something resonate between them that was difficult to describe, but which quickly grew and was related to a desire for destruction, for murder, for breaking a body. They had just wanted to scare an Ybür, to humiliate and doubtlessly molest one, but, now, everything indicated that they were going to turn their victim into a mass of inert, dismantled meat, with neither consciousness nor life.

My father had been socially reinserted a year ago, setting aside, at Granny Holgolde's advice, all politico-military activity, but this retirement weighed on him. I suppose that after having spent a period of his existence eliminating individuals directly participating in human suffering, it is difficult to remain passive in a society where the Werschwell Fraction calls the shots.

The two men hadn't noticed my father, or they took him for a negligible witness they could always deal with later. The wrestler had pushed my mother against one of the trailer's wheels and was kicking her in the stomach, head, and arms. My mother was squirming, crouched in an unfavorable position that didn't allow her to stretch out her right leg and reach her assailant's testicles. The nervous wounded man had finally shut up, and, his cheeks glistening, he was coming around the trailer to seize my mother by the shoulder, or to grab her hair or throat.

My father caught up with this second animal at the moment when he was leaning over my mother and, using the handle of his screwdriver, struck him as hard as he could. Breaking a man's neck in one fell swoop demands an intricate understanding of the human skeleton, married to a perfect mastery of martial techniques. My father possessed this understanding, he had this mastery. The man collapsed onto the tricycle without making a sound, though his fall was noisy and chaotic, accompanied by the flipping of the trailer and squealing of all the metal joints. Even a scrapped doorbell rang during the brief flurry. The larger man paused his beating and turned toward my father, but, before he realized what was happening, my father flipped his screwdriver around and stabbed him in the temple once, then twice, with the tip.

The man took a step forward, as if he wished to keep fighting, or at the very least express a heinous reproach, but then he stood still, his arms hanging alongside his body. He no longer moved. Then his legs faltered, his torso sagged, and he fell headfirst onto the oily cement that covered the pavement.

With that, the violence came to an end.

For about twenty seconds, everything was calm. If anyone was still breathing, it could no longer be heard. Neither my father nor my mother could hear the sounds of their bodies.

Then my mother decided that she had remained lying down long enough.

Now, she was getting up.

She dusted off her pants, wiped away the drops of blood splattered on her cheeks, and massaged her aching legs. She still had not truly met my father's gaze.

Now, they began to perceive the sounds of the surrounding world.

There they were, the two of them, breathing heavily, standing over their enemies, who had already breathed their last. And still they hesitated to look each other in the eye.

4.

My father and mother wordlessly dragged the bodies of the two Werschwell Fraction soldiers over to the wrought-iron railing that bordered the Kanal. There was no great distance to cross, but both of them were shaken by what had just happened and the emotion drained them of some of their strength. I think they still hadn't exchanged a single word at this point. They took the corpses from the scene of the fight, deciding it best not to leave them in plain sight, next to the tricycle and the cart. They started with the one who had been disfigured with the blade of scrap. They laid him along the railing, taking care to orient his punctured face toward the Kanal, then, without pausing, they went back for the one who looked like a wrestler and who had pummeled my mother with his feet. My mother was in pain, and she wheezed through her teeth. My father's forehead and cheeks were dripping with sweat. They dragged the heavy cadaver by its arms. This one's eyes weren't closed and its head bobbed, giving it an unfriendly and disapproving appearance. They placed it next to its comrade. They waited several seconds for their heartbeats to calm, and, since nothing within them would calm, they continued their macabre task. They sat the two corpses up, then lifted them and tipped them, one after the other, over the railing.

No one witnessed their struggle. The neighborhood was deserted.

The corpses quickly rolled down the concrete embankment. The slope was steep and the dead men looked like they were in a hurry to reach the Kanal. The wrestler touched the water and slid in, going under without a second thought, but the other cadaver stopped rolling and lolled in a hideous pose, his legs submerged in the basin, his arms raised, his trunk out of the water, as if he wished to embrace the dry world one last time before his disappearance. Then he seemed to refuse to sink, and to the contrary behaved like a drowning victim pulling himself out of the Kanal, taking a moment to rest before resuming his normal activities on solid ground. His head and spinal column formed an unacceptable angle. His slashed face had left a mark on the cement and continued to leak blood.

My father and mother leaned on the guardrail, but they didn't linger to watch this spectacle. As soon as the larger man's body sunk beneath the surface, they turned around and slowly returned to the tricycle and its trailer.

In that moment, my mother felt her legs give out beneath her. She could no longer keep her disgust over what had happened or her fear hidden. She didn't cry, but her breathing suddenly lost its regularity. Rather than holding this woman against himself to reassure her and telling her, for example, that it was all over and everything would be fine, my father turned her around gently. He picked up from her back the cardboard rectangle that the law required her to wear whenever she went out in the streets, and removed it.

This woman is still alive, it read. *Isn't there something abnormal about this?*

Once he had sent the required announcement flying toward the Kanal, my mother regained her cool. She was proud, strong-willed, and couldn't stand her rescuer taking her for a weakling. She in turn detached the announcement suspended between my father's shoulders.

If this man is not yet drowning in a pool of his own blood, it read, *an anomaly has occurred. Whoever is reading this, make things right.*

Then, they stood there for a moment longer, staring at each other.

Very high up in the sky, just beneath the oppressive clouds, seagulls were flying; if they were making any noise, no one could hear them. Then, behind the window of the old restaurant, which at first appeared abandoned but, in reality, a family of refugees had taken shelter in, a baby began to cry.

That's when my parents decided to get married.

The elephant woke, peeled open her beautiful brown eyes, tiny as they were compared to the rest of her body, and observed the space around her. She hadn't had the chance to sleep for quite a long time, and she had almost forgotten what it felt like to emerge back into consciousness after a time of absence. Seven weeks earlier, she had left her last home, and, since then, she had done nothing but walk interminably. And this particular journey seemed more boring and exhausting than the previous ones. Her memory continuously harried her with her growing fatigue, the dreadful monotony of the route, the shadows rubbing against her powerful bare shoulders and stomach. Like always when one undertakes a long voyage into inexistence after one's own death, she had been assaulted by terrible visions. But she had especially suffered from a tenacious insomnia, she hadn't closed her eyes for a second, and, by consequence, she had at no moment known the ineffable pleasure of waking. Now, she was delighting in her return to the world of the senses without realizing the fading of her own consciousness. Well now, she first thought, just when did you sit down, old Marta? Have you lost your head or what? She tried to recall the events that had comprised the seventh week of her path through the land of the neither-living-nor-dead, but nothing in particular came to mind. She wasn't able to conjure up any significant memories. So she focused on the present, on that which was unfolding in the present, both within and around herself. She had reached the black space's exit, she had just crossed the last meters separating her from her new home. Soon she would burst forth into a new, completely unknown world where fate had long reserved a space for her among the adults. There. It was time. She was receiving initial impressions from the outer world that would from now on be her own. At the same time, she was taking possession of her new body.

But this moment of waking did not come with an ineffable pleasure, not at all.

Her retinas captured an initial image, and, about ten seconds later, the message that thundered in her brain warned of danger, immediate and mortal danger. She was running. The outside world was an abomination, and her body, to escape it, was struggling and plunging blindly into the night.

To make matters worse, this time around Marta Ashkarot had inherited a human skin, an experience she had lived through more than once already, which she had never enjoyed and which she enjoyed even less at the present moment. She was now barely a meter seventy in height, with a disheveled mane of black hair and the pitiful face of a panic-stricken woman in her thirties. She was standing unsteadily on two legs, she had no trunk, and her ears were dwarfish stubs that couldn't even move on their own. She had no muscles worthy of the name, and she ran poorly, not to mention the additional discomfort coming from her chest with every step she took. And her nostrils detected the odor of fear in her armpits, her abdomen, and over the rest of the clothed or naked parts of her body. She found herself isolated and jostled among a small group of people, humans as well, or at least appearing as such, who were zigzagging into the flames, pushed forward by the noises and shouts of the pogrom. She had no idea what awaited her in the coming minutes. The street was a battlefield marked by the sound of shattering windows, the whistle of stabbing knives, the muffled hammering of clubs on hands, legs, temples. An unbelievable rumbling of hatred whirled around her like the roar of a great waterfall.

The extermination had started again.

The massacres were continuing once more.

Marta Ashkarot was fleeing along a sloped street between two rows of vandalized houses. She had finally awakened, but her memories of her bleak journey through the Bardo were already lost in the smoke. Everything connecting her to previous experiences and adventures had dissipated from her mind. Something subsisted, it's true, a feeling of avidity and crisis that ordered her to quickly understand the world in which she was now going to carry out a portion of her existence. There was no respite for her to discover her new home at her own pace and build a unique universe of references. She screamed. The empty space in her head was immediately filled with horror, with images of meaningless violence and insanity and her lack of a future. She was running with the others on a sloped street, with other Ybürs, with, on her left and right, burning houses, fallen Ybürs who were still crawling as they burned, Ybürs lying in the gutter who were no longer crawling, no longer moving, as they burned. The sky was black, the electricity had been cut, the only light came from burning structures and living torches. The light was red, the light crackled and twisted over clothing and flesh, or vehicles ablaze, or smoking apartment windows. The light was alive and fickle, and made frightening leaps in intensity, sometimes disappearing completely, as if to express its disgust with the scene and its inhabitants. Then it was reborn, orange and bloodstained, and after a few terrifying seconds of blind running, it allowed once more for trotting or galloping while avoiding obstacles and, more importantly, soldiers from the Werschwell Fraction, allied with the Zaasch Group's militiamen, gesticulating as they laughed wildly, drunk on crime, gross superiority, and alcohol.

Next to Marta Ashkarot was a disheveled young woman who occasionally would draw away to circumvent a flaming car or an Ybür being beaten by murderers, or to avoid slipping on shards of glass in the middle of the street. The elephant could sense this woman even when she didn't see her, and, although she did not recall having any sort of friendly or even neighborly relationship, she behaved as if the two had been close for quite a long time and as if, in the current catastrophe, they shared a bond of solidarity.

Whenever the woman fell behind, Marta Ashkarot would slow a little to let her catch up.

Both of them were out of breath.

They soon arrived at a large square, a place where the pogrom had not yet reached the height of its furor. Marta Ashkarot crossed the dark space, which seemed nearly silent after the din she had just left. A few forms moved in the shadows, criminals were at work here too, but they were fewer in number than elsewhere. She looped back around to avoid a quartet of soldiers attacking an indistinct mass. Still followed by the disheveled woman, she dove into an alleyway that appeared to be completely deserted. There was a light glowing on a storefront, the power was still on in this sector. Without slowing, they reached the entrance to a small apartment building. They pushed open the door and flattened themselves against the wall. Out of clumsiness, while searching for something with her hand, Marta Ashkarot pressed a button, and the automatic lights switched on. The corridor was cluttered with a jumble of gas meters and mailboxes. Stretched all across the ceiling were cracked pipes, out of which seeped black foam and excremental stenches. The floor's tiling was filthy and, farther in, the wooden staircase's first few steps appeared to have been smashed with a hatchet. Then the lights went out.

They had walked a meter and were now leaning against the mailboxes. In the humid darkness that surrounded them, they listened to the sounds and clamors of the pogrom that suddenly seemed far in the distance. They stayed there, flank against flank, taking the time to catch their breath. Their hair and clothes gave off a dirty steam.

"We're not far from the Party arsenal," the woman finally said in an exhausted voice.

"You know where the arsenal is?" Marta Ashkarot asked, stunned.

"Of course," the woman said. "At the end of the corridor. Where the stairs begin, there's a door that looks like it goes into a closet."

"Let's go," Marta Ashkarot said.

"If we don't give them the code, they won't let us enter," the woman said.

"Do you know it?"

"Know what?"

"The code. Do you know the code?"

"Yes."

"Good. Let's go to the door and you knock."

They groped their way to the staircase. They didn't want to switch on the lights again. Almost undetectable beneath the steps, in a recess that the light would never have reached anyway, the arsenal entrance was small and discouraging. The woman knocked three times quickly in succession, then once loudly, followed by a pause, then she began again. After the third set, the guard opened the door. A lightbulb shone wanly behind his back. It was a man in his fifties. His face was covered in soot, and, like a miner coming out of a mine, his eyes looked abnormally white.

"You've arrived just in time," he said in a predominantly pan-icked tone. "They're getting close to the courtyard exit. Do you have the munitions?"

"What munitions?" the woman asked.

"You didn't bring anything?" the man asked sadly.

Marta Ashkarot shrugged.

"We better come in and close the door," she said. "You can see the light from the street. No need to attract attention."

Once inside, they looked at each other awkwardly. The guard did nothing to mask his disappointment.

"I thought you were coming with cartridges," he deplored once again while shaking his head.

The three of them found themselves in the darkness of a nook that served as a wardrobe. An oily smock and a black coat were hanging on the wall, taking up nearly the entire space. From there, they slipped behind a stack of empty cardboard boxes, after which they were in the arsenal's main room, a not particularly large room to tell the truth, whose only furniture was a mattress lying on the tiled floor, some plastic bags filled with crumpled laundry, and two stools. Behind a screen made of juxtaposed planks, one could just make out the outline of a toilet bowl. A metal sink had been installed just beside it. Near the sink were some hanging towels, tin cans, a saucepan on a portable stove, and two rifles. The room was both livable and lived in.

Marta Ashkarot quickly took note of her surroundings, then lowered her eyes to the mattress and its occupant.

Under the bare lightbulb lay a gravely wounded man. His face was hidden beneath a smoke-stained shirt, and, underneath, he was shivering. A blanket was partially wrapped around his body. His legs stank of charcoal and roasted flesh.

"Who's that?" the woman asked.

The wounded man began to moan. He was conscious. He tried to speak from beneath the shirt covering his face, but his lips and mouth had to be in a deplorable state, and, once he had realized that his words were incomprehensible, he stopped.

"That's the military branch director," the guard said. "He was doused in gasoline, but he managed to escape and come here."

The wounded man tried to say something else. He made an effort to articulate distinctly.

"Do they have the cartridges?" Marta Ashkarot interpreted.

"No," the man replied. "It's two woman comrades. They don't have anything."

Marta Ashkarot went to the sink, leaned over the rifles, and examined them without touching. They were Korean rifles, from the time of the Second Soviet Union. She didn't have enough military know-how to verify whether or not they were loaded, but she promised herself she would take one, shoulder it, and use it against any potential assailants, whether monsters from the Werschwell Fraction, barbarians from the Zaasch Group, or soldiers from the Humanist Alliance. She was ready.

"Are they loaded?" she asked.

She turned toward her fighting companions. With every breath he exhaled, the wounded man let out a pained groan. Above him, the arsenal guard looked worried sick, and his pants were damp with urine. The woman who had run down the street with Marta Ashkarot had taken a few steps away from them, doubtlessly so as not to be contaminated by the despair resonating from the two men. She had stepped over a bag of dirty laundry and was now pressed against the wall, stained with grime, neglect, and an inescapably bleak future. She wasn't completely listless, but scarcely moved. Marta Ashkarot, who until then hadn't had the time to get a look at her face, found her beautiful. She had to be twenty-five or twenty-six years old and, under her common tracksuit, the elephant could make out her perfect, elegant body, not yet ruined by suffering and bloat.

The elephant took the guns, one in each hand, and walked around the mattress, the military director, and the arsenal guard, who was nodding his head like an idiot. She couldn't stop herself from having a sexist thought. It's often that way with men, she reflected. When the situation is a dead end, they don't know what to do.

Then she went to the woman and handed her a gun.

"My name's Marta," she said. "Yours?"

"Joana."

Leading to the courtyard was a small iron door, with, at the top, a grated skylight protected by an interior shutter. The noises outside had increased. The pogromists were invading the neighborhood they had left abandoned for the past half hour. They had spread to the adjacent street and, now that they were approaching the courtyard, Marta Ashkarot could hear their excited voices, the clamor of shattering windows, and the cries of people who had spent the evening playing dead in the shadows. They were being dragged out of their homes and beaten.

"We need to turn off the lamp," Joana ordered.

The arsenal guard leapt toward the switch without a word, and they were suddenly plunged into a heavy darkness, to listen carefully to their loathsome reality and remain silent.

There was a minute of respite.

The wounded man no longer emitted any sound. He had perhaps already died. The guard was at his bedside, his audible breathing interspersed with sobs of helplessness.

In the street, the Zaasch Group soldiers were banging on closed doors and ordering anyone on the other side of them to open up.

Then several criminals burst into the courtyard, and blows reverberated against the skylight and the iron panel. For one reason or another, doubtlessly because they had noticed a trickle of light before, the soldiers knew that the building was occupied. Judging from the voices, there had to be a half dozen of them. Several were exchanging brief humanist considerations on the current action, while others were bellowing loudly.

"They're not loaded," the arsenal guard muttered.

"What?" the elephant asked.

"The rifles," the man said. "They're not loaded."

His voice was at odds with the din outside and the increasingly loud knocks on the door.

"Oh," the elephant commented.

"Don't be scared, Marta," Joana said. "We'll bash their heads in with the grips."

"Oh yes," Marta Ashkarot said. "That's what we'll do. We'll go on the offensive. We'll bash their heads in with the grips."

Granny Holgolde's Tale: The End

Marta Ashkarot realized that someone had stumbled over the threshold of the little house where she had slept through the morning, and then heard a hand or paw pressing urgently against the doorframe. After that, there were several seconds of silence, followed by the sound of fingers knocking on the wooden panel. At first, she had turned her head toward the door, but made no other movement, flabbergasted as she was, since she still couldn't believe her ears. Fingers! A hand! Hominians have a way of knocking on wood that can't be confused with any other animal, even though Marta Ashkarot had been certain that humanity, in this part of the world just as everywhere else, had gone completely extinct. She had lived here for the past four years, ranging over long distances, and not once, in all this time, had she come across representatives of the old dominant species. For a moment, she thought she was still dreaming, but then, once more, human bones, which she also assumed were covered in skin, briefly drummed against the panel so as to announce their presence.

The knocks were lacking in energy.

There was nothing imperious or formidable about them at all.

The elephant groaned two syllables to announce that she was coming to open the door, then pushed away the blanket under which she had spent the night. Hay and vegetable litter rustled around her. Whenever she chose to hole up inside a dwelling, she always brought some things with her to make the stay a little less uncomfortable. This helped her to then collapse until morning without bruising herself too much on the painfully vertical and horizontal surfaces that evolved bipeds were once so fond of, back when they still built houses. Her body had aged, she was made aware of this at the slightest provocation, and there were times when the thought of sleeping on hard ground displeased her greatly. She felt she was approaching the end, that she was now passing through her final existence. And so she allowed herself a morsel of softness. She wasn't proud of this, but, considering the circumstances, she wasn't ashamed of it either.

She stood and gazed at the light emerging from the tiny window. Rather than a proper house, this was a log cabin, a robust and poorly lit construction, conceived to fight back against assaults of cold and snow, a little izba that bore witness to ages long past, since for many decades, even in the farthest reaches of the north, glacial wind and vigorous winters belonged solely to legend. Let's be more precise. They would have belonged to legend if there were still individuals capable of preserving collective memory and making sagas or fables out of it. But no one wandered the earth anymore, no one recounted the past, and no one remembered anything of what had happened. This izba no longer had any reason to exist or story to tell. The elephant had moved in because she had come across it while on her journey and because she felt too exhausted to look for better shelter, but she hadn't given any thought to the people who built it, let alone the climatic conditions that explained the stinginess of its dimensions and its poor lighting.

She opened the door. Since she didn't wish to remain inside the uncomfortable dwelling, she squeezed through the door frame, crossed the threshold, and went outside, in the process shoving aside the two people standing there. She walked about ten meters through the warm grass before turning around to greet her visitors.

They were a hominid couple dressed in rags. Both were in their forties, which indicated that they possessed a nearly miraculous aptitude for endurance, but they both looked quite decrepit and, despite their robust constitution, it was obvious that they were at their physiological limits. The man the elephant had shoved had fallen across the threshold and was making little effort to get back up. The woman, leaning against the izba's exterior, stared at Marta Ashkarot with both steadfastness and exhaustion. Her features betrayed an immense lassitude. The two of them, man and woman alike, had faces matching the situation, the hard and dirty faces of survivors.

The man's hands trembled. He began to grab onto the logs in order to wrest himself into a vertical position. He moved slowly to save his strength. Finally, he leaned his body beside the woman's. Then he searched for her hand and held it in his own.

Now all three of them were staring at one another. The elephant swung forward and back and let her trunk dangle lazily beneath her mouth. The two hominids were holding hands as their lungs produced asthmatic whistlings in cadence. It wasn't clear whether they were considering their words to engage in conversation, or if they were simply thinking about their physical distress and how not to be drowned and asphyxiated by it.

The woman controlled her wheezing and closed her eyes in order to gather a bit of additional strength.

"Is the meeting cancelled?" she finally articulated.

What meeting? Marta Ashkarot wondered.

She had been kicked out of the Party a century ago, for her complacency regarding the theses of adventurists, and, since she never expressed the desire to be reintegrated, the broken bond had never been fixed, and the meanings transformed in her memory into a kind of folklore that no longer concerned her.

"Why?" she asked.

The two vagrants struggled to move their lips, but only the woman was in any sort of state to make sounds.

"The quorum," the woman explained. "We won't be able to make it."

This was no organizational secret, but Marta Ashkarot had the impression that she had weighed the pros and cons before revealing the reason for the plight. It was however already known that the Party was undergoing a serious crisis.

A minute passed. The three were silent and didn't move.

"If you want," Marta Ashkarot finally proposed out of compassion, "we can hold a meeting here, just the three of us."

The vagrants' expressions didn't change. They had the look of people who have faced adversity so often that their flesh has, little by little, turned to wood, their minds ensconced in a hermetic shell that isolates them from ordinary emotions. Marta Ashkarot's proposition was unexpected and potentially lifesaving, but still they expressed no surprise.

"This will be the final one, then," the man spoke up.

"Well, we'll see about that," the elephant replied.

She knew that with hominids, it was always necessary to maintain hope, even if it was uninspired and artificial, and especially when the absence of all hope was particularly flagrant.

The couple didn't react, but she could tell that they were reinvigorated. She took advantage of the situation to treat herself to an observation of her surroundings.

It was a summer morning. Birch trees surrounded the house in an anarchic fashion and, further afield, there were the barely visible curves of hills covered in straw. Since the preceding century, plants had given up on strong, vibrant colors, and changed between faded yellows and uncertain grays, although, that said, they didn't appear unhealthy. Unlike more evolved living organisms and animals, they had found within themselves the resources to adapt to the molecular alterations of the atmosphere and earth. The landscape, in this part of the countryside, continued to play its role, producing tranquility and beauty.

"What is the agenda?" the woman asked.

"Are you talking to me?" Marta Ashkarot inquired.

"Well yes," the woman said.

The elephant heaved her powerful shoulders. She hadn't participated in any kind of political activity for the past ninety-four years and hadn't cared about any kind of agenda since the meeting where, her expulsion for ideological divergence notwithstanding, the plan had been to discuss the emerging conditions of the disappearance of living species. She dug deep into her memory and the title of the discussion returned word-for-word to her tongue.

"Universal happiness in an unfavorable global context," she responded.

"Wait," the woman remarked. "That's exactly the reason we were going to hold the meeting, before it was cancelled."

"Only the Party cares about that theme," the man commented, suddenly distrustful. "Are you a member of the Party?"

The elephant lifted her trunk, scratched herself lightly behind the ear, and let it fall back down.

"These questions come up with some regularity in the Party," she responded.

"So you're a Party member then," the man said, reassured.

"I used to be," Marta Ashkarot replied. "I was a member before your parents were born."

"Good," the woman judged in a breath. "It's better that way. We're among our own kind."

"Yes," the elephant said. "We're among our own kind."

She had pity for the two, who had held fast despite the suite of new historical, chemical, and genetic syntheses. Two individuals who had received at birth, by pure chance, an exceptional capacity for endurance, and whose fate had been to survive, even while everyone else had long disappeared. Two beings whose singular presence against the wall of squared trunks appeared almost heroic, even if their heroism wasn't the result of a personal choice.

She took a few steps forward. Before starting the meeting, she wanted to take them to the spring just behind the house. The water was fresh and abundant, it ran into a slate basin, and, to make use of it, a ladle and bucket were provided. They could have a drink, recover a bit of their strength, and relax.

At that instant, the sky began to rumble and, instead of making their way to the water, they lifted their heads.

There were no objects flying above them, obviously. No machines had skimmed the clouds in eons. Militaries had lasted much longer than humans, but, in their pressurized chambers and environmental suits, they had ultimately run afoul of the fate shared by all—they had ceased to live. Even if a few remaining pilots were still capable of some tiny scrap of organic activity from within their earthbound planes, they certainly didn't have the power to go out and spread flames or viscous gas among the last holdouts of the global population. These lethal missions were now at odds with the deaths of the killers just as much as with the disappearance of their targets.

The sky rumbled continuously across its entire span, throughout its entire depth, and this vibration was completely unrecognizable. It wasn't deafening. It even had a certain gentleness to it.

The fabric's coming undone, Marta Ashkarot thought. The fabric of the universe. It's coming undone. It's destroying itself. The end is very near.

The countryside was calm. If there had still been birds or little wild mammals, one would have perhaps witnessed an animal panic, distraught cries, a hysterical exodus of rats and rabbits. But the countryside was empty and nothing of the sort came to pass. The birches weren't disturbed by a single breath. The morning was gray, cloudy, and warm, like usual. And, up above, the sky was rumbling.

"What's that?" the woman asked worriedly.

"Are you talking to me?" the elephant asked.

"Yes," the woman murmured with effort.

"It's the end," Marta Ashkarot said.

"The end of what?" the woman murmured again.

"I don't know," the elephant said. "The end of the world. Soon there'll be nothing anymore. Nothing. No memories to speak of, no memories to listen to."

The three of them were silent. If there was anything they were trying to imagine, it wasn't the end of the world, with which they were already quite familiar. It was what would come after.

Curiously, after all the years and existences marked by degradation and agony, things at this particular moment were rather peaceful. The sky continued to vibrate and rumble, but the noise suddenly stopped and an intense feeling of relief descended on the three characters. They had arrived at the end of a road, they were entering an image, and the sentiment that had engulfed them was, for all three, more or less the same: they had accomplished their duty as living beings in coming this far, and, now, they were free.

Now, they found themselves gathered in a sort of final photograph, and, when everything ends, it isn't really so bad, especially since this photograph wasn't frightening at all—to the contrary, to them it was incredibly harmonious.

The trunks of the birch trees were lit from the east by an orange glow that could, in a pinch, have been the rising sun, but in reality was simply the world in its final instant. The color intensified, originating from inside the trunks, until it became a brilliant shade of vermilion, then it stabilized. It didn't dull, it didn't grow, shining out from the sapwood, and, throughout the entire forest, there was a luminescence as incongruous as it was beautiful, as if the heart of all matter had been replaced by embers, as if it were a phenomenon completely unfettered by destruction and sorrow.

Universal happiness in an unfavorable global context, Marta Ashkarot thought. Here it is.

She was happy to be frozen in a magnificent end of the world devoid of violence.

The noise from the sky had not returned. The world no longer existed. The birches were consumed from the inside. Matter had dissolved. The countryside was eternally matinal, unmoving, and warm.

The two humans were holding hands. They were leaning against the world's last house, they were resting on the dark logs of the izba and staring out with the hard and dirty faces of survivors.

Everyone was for one final moment immobile inside this final image. The image was going to disappear.

The image disappeared. The luminous red persisted within the retinas, causing the viewer to think once more on the trees, the earth, the inner fire. Then one of the three opened their eyes again, and saw that the red was still there, as a clear and natural reality, at least on the birch trunks, on the earth. Then, from reality's point of view, it was the end.

Memories

Like your hair, like your face, the street is in flames. The situation is hopeless, the pain unbearable, your disgust for the world has reached a limit beyond which you can only manage a brief and terminal scream, but you wait. You are certain that there will be an end. You know that this end is bound to come.

The window facing you opens and shuts, blown by the wind from the fire, as if Maryama Adougaï's arm were shaking it in agitation. The window facing you opens and shuts, swung by the wind from the fire, from the incendiary breaths whirling outside the building. Everyone understands that it is only a playful current of air, that nothing other is intervening, especially not the hand of an animal or human. But each time the window moves, our hearts leap. The window opens and shuts, sometimes violently, and we jolt with the worst images in our heads, as if Maryama Adougaï's caramelized arm really were over there, actively shaking it back and forth.

The glass ended up exploding and, in the frame, several glass shards persevere, like solidly ingrained teeth, like soot-stained fangs, ungleaming. The flames create smoke, the smoke creates fragments that flit up to the middle of the street then fall. What is happening inside the building, just behind the window, cannot be seen.

A rag, the color of a burgundy mop, comes into view. It clings to a piece of glass or a nail. It won't have enough time to fly away from the flames. For half a minute, it appears as if someone is standing near the opening and is using it, this rag, to signal their presence. But this is not the case. No one is standing there. The rag is like many of us, in that it has no chance of escape. Something painful is holding it back, kept inside the blaze, a makeshift hook, an unfortunate hook. For half a minute, we think of it, of this rag. We think of it and we watch it. It does its best to last. It quivers. It quivers and writhes between two jets of smoke. Then it goes up in flames.

The wall does not split quickly. We are there, it is very dark. All paths are blocked, the air is unbreathable. The air no longer exists. Our tears do not reach the edge of our cheeks. They evaporate halfway or are absorbed by the dust. We are not crying over our ruined fate, over the death we now must face much too soon, in the flower of youth. We are not lamenting for so little. If we are crying, it is because our eyes sting. The smoke has thickened, it carries with it acidic substances. In the weak light, we passively examine the fissuring wall. The cracks are taking time to branch outward. They appear and divide slowly. We do not see much, and neither do we have any desire to see what is happening. The air no longer exists, the light is irregular. We are no longer crying. No, we are no longer crying. We remain for a moment with our eyes closed. Everything is too hot. Then, we watch the wall once more. Inside the cracks, the paint forms blisters, and, around the blisters, something hisses. We do not cry, but we do close our eyes.

The pain. We cannot bear it. The Tibetans in the barracks claimed that it could be overcome. They evoked paradoxes, they spoke of religious mantras, three or four elementary indications to put an end to or cope with suffering. But they themselves remained skeptical. In practice, no formula is applicable. We suddenly find ourselves in the heart of pain, we are not even rendered unconscious, to the contrary, we are very awake. We are in the heart of a chain of sufferings. Horribly awakened, suddenly horribly aware of every millimeter of our bodies, of every milliliter of our liquids. And we cannot bear it.

Sleeping in the fire, sleeping in the depth of misery, sleeping in the stones, sleeping finally in a dream of victory, sleeping finally in a dream of eternally fixed time, sleeping finally in the heart of Granny Holgolde's tales, sleeping in death, sleeping endlessly in non-death, sleeping without knowing the extinction of the others, sleeping with our sisters, sleeping with our favorite animals, sleeping without division, sleeping while sharing our bodies with the rest of the world, sleeping while forgetting, sleeping while remembering everything down to the smallest detail, sleeping with you, sleeping in the depths of the black space, sleeping no more, sleeping never again, lying down with the flames, lying down beside the flames, living infinitely and until the end, no longer making any distinction between sleep and life, sleeping until waking, sleeping in the skin of a strange cormorant, waking and living once more in the skin of a strange cormorant, just like in Granny Holgolde's tales, just like in reality.

Imayo Özbeg struggled to get back up on his knees, but he finally did so and took his place again near the window. There was an explosion, perhaps a box of cartridges or a propane tank. His left arm was hanging, unresponsive to any demand and sending him no signal of any sort. His shoulder joints gave him a burning sensation, but he couldn't determine whether or not the arm continued to be bound to his body. If everything there had been severed or torn off, he wouldn't have noticed. I'll worry about that later, he thought. It's not important right now, he thought. Not as important as this. The smells of scorched hair, of fat, of burnt animal fat, of linoleum on fire, had invaded his nostrils. They were powerful but did not nauseate him. To the contrary, even, he received them as if they were an invigorating, revivifying waft. The annulment of opposites, he thought. High and low are superimposed, before and after are no longer differentiated, pestilences and perfumes are equivalent. He remembered the lessons of the Tibetans from the barracks. Opposites turn into nothing more than an indistinct mush, he thought. He pressed himself against the tears in the brick and raised his pistol, as though up toward the sky. On the other side of the street, figures appeared and disappeared according to the goodwill and movements of the smoke. They could not be identified. Friends or enemies, he thought, with a certain gentleness. Faces of friends or enemies. They are joining together. Beneath his eyelids the flames were crackling and nothing could be seen. I can't see anything anymore, he thought. His hand didn't tremble and, if in the distance there really were enemy combatants, he could have targeted and hit them, he could have and anyhow should have shot them to show that he was no weakling, but he held back. Perhaps he was a weakling, after all. He breathed in a large gulp of air and was greeted with an abominable stench of carbonized flesh, of bodies in ovens, and suddenly he thought that it may be his own flesh, his own body, that was coming undone in the flames. Oh, he thought. For a moment that was all he could think. Oh, he thought again. That's all I can think. I really am a weakling.

At your feet the linoleum suddenly splits open and releases a jet of red, oily, repugnant vapor. You take a step backward. You are not yet used to walking through fire. You have difficulty admitting that you are no longer Maryama Adougaï, that already you have transformed into a giant and strange cormorant. The Tibetans had warned you, and Granny Holgolde had often mentioned it in her stories. You are dead, you are not dead, you are walking through fire. The linoleum resembles hardened magma, it emits toxic gasses, it emits an indescribable fetidity, the air is boiling, the walls flutter like sails in the wind, colors and darkness cancel each other out, you advance inside the orange, you traverse shades of red and orange previously unknown to you, camphromander, light mizerine, uldamor. You advance through stopped time, you are not yet completely aware that you have become a strange cormorant, you are not yet convinced that you will live forever in the fire and without any pain, the idea still seems too unfamiliar to you, too incongruous, too extravagant, but this is because you are still the memory of Maryama Adougaï. You are still the memory of Maryama Adougaï. That is correct, yes. You are already a strange cormorant, you are no longer Maryama Adougaï, but you are still her memory.

Among all Granny Holgolde's tales, some were more marvelous than others. She places in them strange cormorants who appear to be returning from their committee work, who appear to be leaving administrative buildings dedicated to the fight against enemies of the people, against saboteurs of the five-year plan, against representatives of the seventh, eighth, and ninth stinking categories. The strange cormorants can also be found on liquidation missions, where they are much darker and, beneath their raincoats or feathers, they carry weapons. They are dressed in leather jackets, as in the time of the First Soviet Union, or they have put on camouflaging rags, as in the time of the Second Soviet Union, or they have no clothing, and they go naked, covered in feathers, indifferent to the cold, damp, and wind, as if resembling humans no longer interests them at all. According to Granny Holgolde, according to her fanciful sayings, perishing in fire during combat opens the door to an immediate metamorphosis into a strange cormorant. Our childhood was awash in such nonsense. I remember the shining eyes of Drogman Baatar, of Ouassila Albachvili, of Taïa Torff, whom we called Chicha. Those of Laura Gheen, who wasn't mute but never spoke, drowning in tears of impatience. She had trouble understanding that this promise of transformation could only come to pass after many long years, after childhood and adolescence and after a terrible sacrifice, and that perhaps, for her, the opportunity would never arise.

You stretch your right wing toward the ceiling. Apart from yourself, everything is more or less frozen. The fire changes very slowly. The sparks are suspended between sky and earth, floating lazily, indecisive in their trajectory. The torches resemble untouched tapestries and veils. You shake your wings as if to dry them after a plunge into the waves, but the rest of the world is immobile. The interior of the blaze, anyway, seems fixed on one image. The flames do not propagate, they do not dance, they twist slowly, they do not move. In the very immediate vicinity, just around you, they still manifest as animated, whispering creatures, in bubbles and jolts, but, if we consider the entire warehouse, we can say that they are completely paralyzed. Your name is Maryama Adougaï, you are in the center of the blaze, on the ground floor of the Kam Yip Building. You have been dispossessed of all hope since your birth, you are currently burnt to the bone and struck mute, dispossessed of all known life, and, in order to assess your new appearance, you are stretching your right wing toward the ceiling, and, with no consequence other than a light warmth, you touch the cluster of flames formed there, unmoving or moving incredibly slowly, so beautiful that you suddenly want to sob, so beautiful that you sob, though perhaps you are also moved by your own fate and by the apocalyptic dimension of our defeat, of your defeat, yours and the others', which has always been there, since your birth, since always.

One after the other, you each hatch in the fire, surviving for a moment with horrible burns and covered in ashes. You have become monsters, invisible to the human eye. Only children can believe in you now, or at least those who have heard Granny Holgolde's tales. Who else would imagine your birth within the flames, your tranquility amid the blaze? One after the other you each leave your charred skin behind and rise, sighing, you stretch your wings which do not ignite, you become aware of your beak, your feathers. You are alone. You are absolutely alone. The fire is frozen around you. Everything is immobile. A strange existence awaits you, inside a moment where time has been erased. A perpetual moment with neither duration nor change. You have life, but nothing else. And what happens when the fire dies? Imayo Özbeg thinks, with a feeling of spite that he cannot control. What happens when we no longer have the flames for companions?

You feel as though you have fallen asleep and that much time has passed during your slumber. You recall that in the moment when you closed your eyes, a ball of flames was falling, accompanied by a corona of sparks. Just below, four meters down, Drogman Baatar was lazily sprawled, his mouth twisted into a curse he had refrained from uttering, his legs bathed in tar or blood. The fiery mass had chosen him as its target. And you, at this moment, you have closed your eyes and quickly dozed off, and, now, without a start and without transition, you are waking up. You open your eyes and the ball of fire has not reached its goal, it is now halfway there and resembles a ferocious, disintegrating comet with a disorganized tail. You think: "What will happen once it all stops burning?" And you want to go back to sleep.

With great slowness, one after the other, clusters of orange fire detach from the ceiling and, after passing through vertical space, explode below and spread, on the ground, on the heaps of dirty, useless clothes, feeding on cadavers, and also on confiscated objects, radio sets, televisions, drums, phonographs, Bakelite rollers, ebonite discs, chairs, vinyl discs, books, soldier's coats, spring coats, winter coats, broken rifles, torn underclothes, incomplete sets of tableware, Mongolian felt bags, leather bags.

I do not know what you are thinking, but for me, waking up as a bird in the middle of an inferno would be a little frightening.

Waking covered in feathers, inside a scene of half-petrified flames. Yes. That would frighten me at least a little.

The solitude would, as well. Knowing that we're going to exchange a few sentences from time to time with the others, over an incredibly long span, but that at heart we will remain ensconced in the depths of our feathers, with nothing else to do, or only minor tasks, until the end of the inferno, which we will never see.

Furthermore, no one has ever returned to describe what things are like on the other side. From this point of view, and it could only be from this point of view, the entire process is suspect. It's understandable that communication would be difficult. But all the same, there has been no manifestation of any sort to confirm that it's anything more than just a legend, a simple legend born from Granny Holgolde's imagination.

It seems that one does not even get the choice of bird. It's either transform into a strange cormorant, or nothing. Take it or leave it.

Leaving behind your charred or soon-to-be-charred cadaver, standing in the middle of the flames, ruffling your feathers, and living forever within an inferno, and discovering that all the men and women who've survived now look like strange cormorants, and realizing that there is no way back, take it or leave it, and having confusedly lost your identity to the point that you're no longer certain if your name is Rita Mirvrakis, Elli Zlank, or Drogman Baatar. I don't know about you, but for me, this would make me feel very uncomfortable.

Imayo Özbeg gave us the agreed-upon signal and we split apart from the Bolcho Pride parade. My heart was racing and, at the same moment, I felt as though the sky had suddenly turned dark. "Did you see that?" I asked Dariana Freek. "What?" "The sky!" She lifted her head. "I don't see anything," she said nervously. "From now on, I won't even look at the sky anymore!" I didn't know how to interpret her response. Was she afraid? Was she about to confront something much worse than a simple combat mission? Was she thinking about what would come after our raid, our failure, our death, about the reprisals against the survivors? "It's very dark," I said. "What is?" she asked. "The sky," I explained. "It's very dark."

"I don't like the sky's color," Baatar Drogman, at my side, declared. "What does it mean?" Taïa "Chicha" Torff asked. "Is it a bad omen?" Drogman Baatar stopped walking. He faced Taïa Torff as if he wanted to block her way or fight her. "From now on," he said, "only rely on bad omens. There's nothing else in our future." "Does that mean the sky's a bad omen?" I asked. He glared at me, but then his eyes sparkled with a kind of joy. "Yes, it is," he said. "It couldn't get any worse!"

It was neither a matter of disobeying the Party, nor of obeying. The Party hadn't been consulted, the Party hadn't been informed, albeit in a devious and indirect way—not even Granny Holgolde, as busy and obsessed as she was with the success of our Bolshevik

Pride parade. We had decided to take action without asking anyone and we still had enough sense of discipline not to let the secret get out, even during the days of exaltation that preceded Bolcho Pride.

Granny Holgolde has always treated us like her children, like her dragons, and, after this catastrophic Bolcho Pride, she was overwhelmed with compassion and indulgence, and she continued to see us in the same light. We remained in her memory as her heroes and heroines, as her unfortunate daughters and sons, as secret and tender figures, as strange and immortal cormorants. She thus defended us tooth and nail when the Party wished to posthumously expel us. She wasn't able to prevent our expulsion, but she resolutely pleaded our case. "Don't worry, little ones," she said, looking toward the smoke and the black sky. "It's just a matter of time. Once the world revolution has triumphed, I'll get you reintegrated into the Party's measly rank and file, fear not!"

During the Party meeting, whose agenda included our condemnation for childish obsession and belonging to several stinking categories, dolls made in our effigy were presented before the Commission and successively pelted with terrible reproaches. In the interests of equity, those who wished to defend our cause, or at least soften the ideological blows, were invited to stand behind the dolls and speak in our stead. Only Granny Holgolde took part in this exercise. She left her seat, hobbled over to the doll representing me, and said: "I know that we have come to odds with the Party's anti-adventurist traditions, and with iron will we have all accepted and extolled as a fundamental principle the centuries of intense battles and defeats. I know this, I derive no pride from it, and I don't care."

Granny Holgolde next placed herself behind the doll representing Taïa "Chicha" Torff and spoke on her behalf: "We have absolutely not called materialism into question," she said. "At no time have we ever believed in the presence of strange cormorants, either in reality or in our dreams."

The parade had disappeared behind us, but we could still hear the roar of slogans, the crowd shouting slogans for the immediate uprising of the masses, the suppression of the world of camps and the immediate construction of a universe where our enemies would dwindle in camps until their definitive extinction, the creation of a radically egalitarian, fraternal, liberated, and intelligent society, the hanging of those responsible for the Zaasch Group, the execution of those responsible for suffering, the dismantling of the Werschwell Fraction's innumerable mobs, the suppression of international charity organizations, the end of wealth and privilege of all kind, the immediate application of our minimum program, and the undelayed implementation of our maximum program.

Drogman Baatar broke the lock and we entered the Kam Yip Building. Immediately, we were suffocated by the smell of gasoline, so heavy that it was as if it had replaced all the oxygen in the room. We were expecting the stench of a waste processing plant, but if, beneath the musty odor, the presence of repugnant materials, foul leathers, and fatigued paperwork truly existed, it was all overwhelmed by the fuel.

The Kam Yip Building had been a multilevel store half a century ago, before the part of the city it served was enclosed into the ghetto, and, little by little, it found itself surrounded by dilapidated and uninhabitable constructions. The authorities made a warehouse out of it to hold furniture, objects, and weapons confiscated from the surrounding area and even from much farther away, from the Amaniyak Kree District, Bloc 709, and even the Vincents-Sanchaise Zone or the ghettos to the northwest whose names were unknown to us. Soldiers from the Werschwell Fraction and auxiliaries would come from time to time to arm themselves, but, once everything that had been valuable or of high quality was gone, hobbyist pillagers became rare. The ambience of piles of garbage had taken over most of the building, which had completely taken on the aspect of an abandoned pigsty. There were guards who surveilled the place, but without much diligence or any dogs, and one could sense that it was an institution at the end of its life. I don't know who among us claimed that one day or another, the authorities would set it on fire just to get rid of the thing. We had difficulty taking that hypothesis seriously, since we believed that the heaps, disorder, and architecture of the place would complicate the undertaking of that sort of villainy.

What brought us inside the building was the section of the warehouse where the weapons were kept. Of course, we knew that the arsenal's cabinets wouldn't contain anything particularly functional, but despite this, we expected to harvest enough ammunition and pistols to take a few spectacular actions against the barracks managers, special sections, charitable institutions, and slaughterhouses. Our plan was simple: break into the Kam Yip Building when all the police forces would be mobilized to direct the Bolcho Pride parade toward avenues with little strategic importance and protect the homes of important personalities that the parade might pass. The day before, Loula Maldarivian had parked a wagon in a neighboring courtyard to transport our spoils, a type of delivery tricycle that was falling to pieces and thus wouldn't risk attracting attention. We thought to act in less than half an hour, cover the requisitioned guns with festive banners, allowing us to pass unnoticed in the streets, and then, with the wagon, rejoin the demonstration and plunge once more into the swell of Bolshevist sympathizers.

We crossed the first twenty meters by zigzagging through the shadows, between mountains of clothes and shoes that stunk of gasoline. We tramped through puddles or over soaked fabrics. "Hey," one of us muttered, "they've emptied out who knows how many jerricans here!" "Another bad omen, I think." "I won't even look at anything anymore," Chicha said. Elli Zlank told us to shut up and pointed to something in a vague direction, wrinkling his face to listen. We were suddenly paralyzed, a frozen group of outcast boys and girls pricking up our ears to catch the noises Elli Zlank had heard. There was nothing in the returned silence for several seconds, except for the Bolcho Pride slogans roaring over the neighborhood, then, at the other end of the building, I distinctly picked up the rattling of metal cans on the ground, followed by the echo of a stream, then a few words, then an uninterpretable scraping, then, once more, a spilling.

This is when we committed our greatest and only mistake. Instead of calling off the operation, instead of hastily retracing our steps, we continued onward up the stairs to the second floor, where we thought the arsenal would be.

We reached the second floor without any problems. The men who were finishing up pouring gasoline all over the ground floor may have heard us, or they may not have. The shouts and slogans of Bolcho Pride may have covered up the sound of our footsteps. They had no intention of going back to the sections of the building they had already taken care of. They must have made sure that none of their own would risk being left behind, and they wanted to leave the premises as quickly as possible. They knew that no one could still be wandering around the warehouse, and if by chance any thieves or basically animal undermen had broken into the building, this could be considered minor collateral damage at most. Any intruders only had themselves to blame if they were overtaken by misfortune.

The sounds made by the fire starters faded once we had forced open the door to the arsenal. We were, it goes without saying, very aware of the danger. But, since nothing yet had happened, we figured we had the time to grab a few armfuls of Kalashnikovs, cartridge boxes, and some pistols dating back to the First Soviet Union before running off. The door finally gave way. We stood just inside the room. It was overflowing with pistols, tossed haphazardly into crates. Some Stechkin-Avramovs, Yariguins, Tokarevs, Makarovs, Serdyukovs, and one Bogdanov. It was difficult to determine whether they were broken or still usable. We had lost half a minute to weighing and examining them, and, as we began to pick up the crates to transport them outside, the fire sparked on the ground floor, and we immediately realized that we could no longer go back downstairs and leave the Kam Yip Building in one piece.

In order to impress the Disciplinary Commission and ensure our rehabilitation, Granny Holgolde went around the trial room and closed the already restrictive openings, and, once everything was plunged into a suffocating darkness, she dragged to the stage a piece of sheet metal. She had gained a lot of weight over the past few years and had difficulty walking, but her obstinance demanded respect and, in her presence, no one made a sound. On the center of the metal, which resembled a small baking sheet, she placed a cloth figure in effigy of Ouassila Albachvili, then she declared that she wished to speak for five minutes in the name of our little sister Ouassila. No one uttered any objection, so she assumed that she had been given the right to do so. She then poured a glass of gasoline over the doll's head and lit the doll on fire. "Finally, I, Ouassila Albachvili, have decided to keep my mouth shut," she said, and then was silent. The Disciplinary Commission didn't know what to do, and its members remained calm, surrounded by the smell of gasoline and char, their eyes watering, their mouths severe, their souls vague, and their breathing constrained.

There were several hearings. They took place sometimes behind closed doors, other times out in the open. When the Commission undertook its work inside some enclosure or another, Granny Holgolde was the sole individual to cross the threshold. Whenever she entered she appeared full of determination and even often on the brink of fury. Her eyes flashed with lightning, and, if there had been any human or animal in her way, it would have moved without further ado. Later, when she came back out, she looked exhausted, crushed by fate, and her disheveled clothes smelled of grease, petrol, and indoor fire.

In the case of certain hearings that took place in public, Granny Holgolde would ask a soldier to push her wheelchair to the Negrini Bloc's barracks for invalids and the mentally ill. Once a compact audience of polytraumatized and schizophrenic individuals had formed before her, she would copy the voice of one or another of us, usually Rita Mirvrakis, whose inflections weren't too different from her own, and she would repeat a few passages from our maximum program. From this she selected sutras that wouldn't risk shocking the masses, then she would recount in her own way the failed operation in the Kam Yip Building, with which she mixed meditations on eternity and certain strange cormorants that she claimed to have seen at several important junctures in centuries past, then, if her oration hadn't yet worn her out, she would declare the hearing adjourned and continue to call out to the masses and speak, this time in her own voice.

It took the ground floor less than ten seconds to transform into a sea of fire. We were cut off from all routes back to the street. Evacuation was now impossible. We leaned over the balcony guardrail to see the extent of the nightmare. A burning heat stung our cheeks and eyelids. "If the Party had been warned," Maryama Adougaï ventured, "they could have saved us from outside!" "The Party no longer exists," Imayo Özbeg remarked. The second floor windows were unopenable. They were placed high up, and most of them were sealed with bricks, iron lattices, or pilings. "Maybe it existed in the past, but today, it's not even in basement thirty-six, it simply no longer exists." Loula Maldarivian then proposed to the girls to make use of the pistols we were going to requisition. "When we're surrounded by fire," she suggested, "when we can't take any more pain and fear, we can use them to kill ourselves." We had agreed, we had turned back toward the arsenal with the thought of gathering any ammunition we could find. Drogman Baatar distributed cartridges to anyone who wanted them. "It was really worth going through all this just to shoot one bullet," Taïa Torff grumbled, then walked away with her Stechkin. I don't know if she later made use of it, if she knew how to release the safety catch, if she pressed the barrel against her throat or beneath her floating ribs.

Granny Holgolde lit a marionette on fire, on which she had inscribed the name Imayo Özbeg, and declared that now through her everyone would hear the voice and explanations of Imayo Özbeg and no one else. The Disciplinary Commission gave her the sign to continue, and she said: "I solemnly affirm that at no moment did I doubt the existence of the Party. It is certain that our general collapse, punctuated here and there by occasional capitulations and lost battles, could have led me to believe that the Party had vanished for good. But I refused to come to that conclusion and, in any case, I kept my opinion to myself and never expressed it aloud, even as I was engulfed by flames."

The boiling smoke had begun to singe the skin on our hands and faces. The hair on some of our heads was beginning to burn. "Do you remember, in Granny Holgolde's tales, when the elephant changed homes?" Dariana Freek asked. "When she took her first steps into the intermediary worlds, and stopped worrying about the horrible past and horrible present?" "No," Loula Maldarivian said. "I don't remember and I don't care."

Once all the dolls representing us had burned, the Disciplinary Commission recessed to deliberate, and, once she was finally all alone, Granny Holgolde collapsed onto the ground. "My dears," she exclaimed, her voice made indecipherable by her sobs, "all my little ones! You burned for nothing! We're all at the bottom of the hole, and the Party doesn't seem to know which direction to go to get out, but, whatever happens, we're all with you!"

A few words now on Ouassila Albachvili, also called, like me, Rita Mirvrakis, and on Loula Maldarivian, whom quite a few people also called Rita Mirvrakis. To say, above all, that within the flames, we were together. The words have no importance, but they exist and they emphasize, in their own way, our closeness within the inferno in the Kam Yip Building. All three of us, for a moment, were together, and what we shared will stay with us like a precious, indestructible jewel of loving friendship. Ouassila Albachvili has, like me, a long black braid that swings against her spine when she walks. She has the looks of a woman from the Caucasus, a superb woman from the Caucasus. Her hair is thick. It descends to the bottom of her back when she moves. It pulls on the top of her forehead and causes her to have a bearing that the guards and teachers always found arrogant and inappropriate. Ouassila Albachvili took advantage of Bolcho Pride to dress up as an outcast Georgian princess, far from everything, magnificent. She still has in her jacket pocket some of the hairpieces that once allowed her to take on the appearance of Dzerzhinsky, hairpieces dating from the time when she was a little girl and which resembled nothing, and obviously very little of Iron Felix's own pilosity. It's no more than a scrap of grimy fiber, an amulet she's saved since the time when her parents foisted

Bolshevik costumes upon her without giving too much thought to whether she would prefer to inhabit the false skin of a man or a woman. With the help of nostalgia, she is like us all, she now thinks that this was a time when the camp knew moments of great joy, and that Bolcho Pride was one of them. It might be doubtful, but that's what she believes, at least when all around us everything is going poorly. She closes her hand on this talisman stuck to the bottom of her pocket along with crumbs of food. She touches it and mumbles the magic spells that Granny Holgolde taught her, calling for the terrible punishment of all those responsible for disaster and all those who obeyed them and who continue to this day to obey them. I am doing the same thing. I, too, curl my fingers around the residue of a distant Pride from my childhood, a strand of Rosa Luxembourg's chignon. I, too, pronounce maledictions. One day the camp authorities, the soldiers of the Zaasch Group, and all those who possess the world will be instantaneously reduced to ghosts, and, if the revolution doesn't take care of it, we can always count on natural catastrophes. This is what my curses prophesize. One day, whatever happens, they will all shrivel up and be ground to tar, nothing more than bad memories. Loula Maldarivian is wearing a buckle from Chapayev's ushanka as a pendant. It is perhaps an homage to Chapayev, perhaps an homage to her little brother, who was killed when he was very young, a few days after having worn this very outfit. Loula Maldarivian's hair is brown like gingerbread and she is wearing generally Mongolian rags, which suit her well, since she is broad-shouldered and has short and solid legs. She lifts her hand to her chest, presses Chapayev's buckle between her breasts, and murmurs one of Granny Holgolde's terrifying prayers. The flames surround us. Already we are together, reunited. But we were also together later. I will speak of it. Later and even more together.

Then Loula Maldarivian falls on me, and for a moment we're lying on top of one another, amid the cracklings and pain. Then

Ouassila Albachvili collapses onto us, onto what remains of us, a sort of indistinct blaze, which hardly moves and no longer vociferates. All three of us are together. We speak our name one last time, Rita Mirvrakis, Rita Mirvrakis, Rita Mirvrakis, then we are silent.

We were surprised by and still little accustomed to our strange bird bodies, little familiar with the prolonging of time and existence inside the fire. I freed myself from the sooty heap we had formed and made my way to the next closest heap, where the most disparate of objects were now neighbors, witnesses to a civilization and culture we had once known ourselves or which had been known generations before, to which we felt a total closeness and solidarity. I pulled from the jumble a record player, I picked it up and placed it on a table so it would be horizontal and secure. I began to examine it, trying to understand how it functioned, if it still possessed a wire and pin to plug into an outlet, when Rita Mirvrakis made a gesture with her fingers, covered in blue, white, and indigo feathers, indicating that the device didn't need electricity in order to work. "In similar circumstances," she claimed in a voice whose intensity shocked me, "no electricity is needed." I had no reason not to believe her. We were stuck in one reality among several others, amid flames that looked like immutable tapestries, and electricity belonged to another world. Electricity could be forgotten, strange magic was our only guide. Rita Mirvrakis was holding a vinyl disc in her hand, which she had just pulled from a pocket, and I saw, according to the Cyrillic characters on the label, that the disc had been pressed during the First Soviet Union. She placed the black circle onto the platter, I moved the arm into place, and the mechanism began to rotate. At the center of the frozen scene, in the heart of this frozen inferno which would forever be our home, this black disc turning at thirty-three rotations per minute was an extraordinary event. I don't know if it could be called a miracle, but, in any case, it made us happy.

I placed the needle on the first black ridge and stepped away. Now all three of us were standing against each other, next to the record player, then we separated slightly and formed a sort of approximative circle around the device's speaker.

The voice belonged to one of the great heartrending singers of the First Soviet Union, Lyudmila Zykina. I don't know what you would have thought of it, in our stead, in the silence of the flames that resembled shining stalagmites. I suppose all the same that you, too, would have been deeply moved. The song was a simple and harrowing melody. A peasant woman has just lost her wedding ring, she finds it, she thinks with sorrow of the man whom she loves and who is now gone. She puts on a white dress and prepares to walk through the snow into the night, hoping for nothing, relying on the moon to light her path. The inferno around us burns very slowly. The torches lazily writhe and sway. The temperature is pleasant. Everything is immobile. We had folded our wings along our flanks and, aware that we too would never again see the man whom we loved, or the snow, or the night, we felt tears run through the down on our faces.

Your name is Maryama Adougaï. You are at the edge of the abyss. Time has cracked around you, space is no more. You would like for me to approach you one last time, to cling to you tightly one last time, for the fear of abandonment and the pain of solitude to diminish. You call out. Time and space are no more, the blazing dark is no more. You say your name, our name, and you call out. You speak our memories, you would like to speak our memories, those which belong to you and those which are buried within others and which they have never told to anyone else. You would like to dig up our memories. You open your mouth, but inside there is no more breath, no more words. You are within the abyss and you call out. No one responds. You spread your wings, you unfurl them, you move the air and the burning shadows around you. You would like to take flight, or at least stay afloat somewhere, between two worlds. You would like to fly and to forget for a very long time.

Your name Maryama Adougaï. I have the same name, too. Many of us are the same, now. This is the end. We all have the same name, all of us. A moment ago, this name was Rita Mirvrakis, but now we are called Maryama Adougaï, all of us, boys and girls alike. You are on the edge of the abyss or have already fallen in. Time has cracked around you, space is no more. You would like for me to approach you one last time, to cling to you tightly one last time, for the fear of abandonment and the pain of solitude to diminish. You call out. Time and space are no more, the flames and the blazing dark are no more. You say your name, our name, and you call out. You speak our memories, those in the light and those which are buried. You would like to cry, but your tears have vanished, there are no more tears or dry eyes. You would like to speak our memories, those which belong to you and those which are buried within others and which they have never told to anyone else. You would like to dig up our memories which have always lain beneath tons of bitumen and earth. You open your mouth, but inside there is no more breath, no more words. You are within the black abyss and you call out. No one responds, not even Maryama Adougaï. You spread your wings, you unfurl them, you move the air and the burning shadows around you. You would like to take flight, or at least stay afloat somewhere, between two worlds. You would like to fly and to forget for a very long time. You would like to glide high above the Kam Yip Building, above the Amaniyak Kree District, above Vincents-Sanchaise Street, like a person who is neither sure she knows how to fly nor sure she wishes to land. You would like to forget everything for a very long time above the washhouse, above Liars' Bridge, above the barbed wire that surrounds Bloc 709 and the Negrini Bloc, above the barracks for invalids and the mentally ill, above the administrative buildings, above the slaughterhouses, above the soldiers, above our cadavers and our memories, reduced to next to nothing. I no longer have the strength to forget, I no longer have the strength to speak to you, but: my memories are yours.

Manuela Draeger is one of French author Antoine Volodine's numerous heteronyms belonging to a community of imaginary authors that includes Lutz Bassmann and Elli Kronauer. Since 2002, she has regularly published novels for adolescents with L'Ecole des Loisirs. *Eleven Sooty Dreams* is her second book to be translated into English.

J.T. Mahany is a graduate of the MA program in Literary Translation Studies at the University of Rochester and received his MFA from the University of Arkansas. His translation of Antoine Volodine's *Bardo or Not Bardo* won the inaugural Albertine Prize in 2017.

OPEN LETTER

WWW.OPENLETTERBOOKS.ORG